CW01574641

More Writing on the Edge

An Anthology of Writing

by the

Wotton Writers Group

Editors:

Anne Sheppard
Caroline Bennett
Jane Gray-Wallis

First published in 2022 by Paragon Publishing Ltd.

ISBN 978-1-78222-965-0

Book design, layout and production management by Into Print
www.intoprint.net
+44 (0)1604 832149

Introduction

Having edited our last anthology (which was published in 2012 and won the NAWG Best Anthology of the Year Award in 2013) I was delighted to hand-over the task of producing this latest anthology to a new and younger team. One of the basic requirements of any successful writing group is the willingness of the group's members to share ideas and work together, and this is exemplified by the editorial team assembled to put this collection of poetry and short stories together. So may I start by thanking Anne Sheppard, Caroline Bennett, and Jane Gray-Wallis for the hours they spent chasing submissions, editing them into a common format, producing contributor biographies, and managing the dozens of other tasks and decisions that are needed to create and publish an anthology like this. They have done a fantastic job.

Of course, any anthology is only a carefully curated selection of the best bits of writing, and for every story published here there are dozens of unfinished pieces and unloved stories. All writers struggle at some point, because they can't see how the story develops, have lost their confidence, or because they simply don't like this month's exercise, but that's OK – it is part of writing, and one of the reasons we set different exercises every month is to help us work through those times by exploring something new, focusing on a particular skill such as dialogue, or just writing something to get past the occasional writer's block. Even if it ends up as a crumpled ball of paper in the waste bin at the end of the evening. Keeping the 'writing muscle' exercised is what's important. So let me thank all of those in the Group who have contributed themes for our monthly exercises, and led the workshops, focus sessions and group exercises that help develop all of us as writers. A good writers group is a powerful ally, whatever you want to write, and I feel privileged to be the Secretary of this special group of people. One day, I'll tell a story I really feel happy with and some of its DNA will have come from this Group.

I hope you enjoy reading this collection and, as always, should you feel inspired to join a writers group, or if you just want to find out more about what we do, please get in contact via our website. Thank you.

Alan Shrimpton
Secretary: Wotton Writers Group
wottonwritersgroup.wildapricot.org

Contents

The Phone Box Club

by Alan Shrimpton

This piece came from a photo exercise. We had to choose a picture from a pile on the table and then create a short story based on our chosen image. I chose a picture of a phone box on a lonely roadside but then struggled to find any inspiration until I googled 'most remote phone box' and the idea of the Phone Box Club was born.

Mark eased the big Volvo around the bend and then accelerated up the incline. The moors of mid-Wales stretched off on either side, bathed in early morning sunshine and long shadows. The sun had only just broken over the eastern hills.

'Almost there,' he said to the woman sitting in the passenger seat and shifting down a gear.

His wife turned away from the view and gave him an appraising look.

'Stop smirking,' she said, though with the trace of a smile.

'I'm not smirking. I'm enjoying this beautiful morning,' said Mark. 'Look Gill,' he waved a hand at the empty landscape stretching away on either side of the car. 'We have the world to ourselves.'

'That's because it's 6:00 a.m. on a Sunday morning,' said Gill. 'I got out of a perfectly lovely bed in Tregaron and gave up my full English breakfast to drive into the back of beyond. I must be mad.'

'It will be fun,' said Mark.

'Will it,' said Gill, her tone indicating that she was not sure it would. Mark powered the car around another bend, attacking the road. She looked at him again. 'Do men ever grow up?'

'Growing old is compulsory, growing up is not,' said Mark. 'I read that somewhere.'

'Hmm,' said Gill. 'On the same website that you got this mad idea from I suspect. But what does that make me for agreeing to it?' She shook her head and returned to gazing out of the car.

'You thought it was a good idea when I suggested it. In fact, I think you said that it was a deliciously wicked idea.' This time he did smirk.

'That's only because you opened that second bottle of Prosecco,' said Gill, 'and I'm sure you did that deliberately.'

'Me,' said Mark, managing to sound hurt whilst grinning hugely. 'I'd never do such a thing.'

'Yes, you would. You've done it before. And I should know better.'

There was silence for a moment.

'Look in the bag,' said Mark.

Gill opened the bag by her feet and pulled out a bottle of Prosecco in a chiller jacket. She saw that there was a carton of orange juice and two glasses in the bag as well.

'Bucks Fizz,' said Mark. 'Breakfast or Dutch courage. You choose.'

Gill shook her head at her husband but giggled at the same time. 'Well, 10 out of 10 for preparation I guess…'

'We're here,' said Mark, clearly delighted. The car crested a ridge and he pulled into the side of the road which dropped away slightly and then divided into a forked junction about 50 yds farther on. A solitary red phone box stood at the junction.

'The most remote phone box in Wales,' said Mark with a satisfied grin, 'miles from anywhere and we have it all to our… *bloody bollocking hell*,' he shouted. 'What's she doing here?'

Mark stared at the phone box as an older lady emerged wearing a high-vis jacket. She began to unroll a large banner and then stretched it between the phone box and a wooden post some 6 feet away.

Gill grinned. The banner read 'Tregaron Moor Cycle Challenge' in big letters and 'CHECKPOINT' in even bigger letters.

Gill laughed at the exasperation on her husband's face.

'It's 6 a.m. on Sunday morning,' he said, hands raised in mute appeal to the universe at the unfairness of it all. 'What on earth is she doing here?'

'Oh, you should see your face,' said Gill.

'It's not bloody fair,' said Mark, thumping the steering wheel. 'Who gets up at this hour on a Sunday morning?'

'Race marshals,' said Gill, gleefully pointing out the obvious. The lady in the high-vis jacket picked up a thermos and began to pour herself a drink.

'Aww, no,' said Mark, 'not today… not after all that planning.'

'Sorry lover,' said Gill, leaning over in her seat to rest her head on his shoulder. 'That's life.'

Mark banged the steering wheel again.

'I guess you'll just have to be satisfied with Mile High Club instead,' said Gill. 'And let's face it, the Phone Box Club doesn't quite have the same ring to it. Does it?'

Narrow Escape

by Dave Beer

Based on a writing exercise which uses Raymond Chandlers' suggestion that if a story has ground to a halt, have a person holding a gun enter the scene.

A streak of iridescent turquoise, more imagined than seen, disappeared into the rushes to find a new perch for spotting breakfast. An arrow of water slid across the canal, pointing the way the water vole had decided best served its unknown purpose. The silence gave way to the buzz of a dragonfly's wings, darting in and out of mist-wreathed weeds in a display of aerobatics worthy of a miniature biplane.

And then another sound, mechanical, heralding the graceful passage of a narrowboat. The gentle rumble of the diesel engine, the tiller light in his hand, the calm of early morning all contributing to a soporific effect on Roger.

The thunderous crash of steel on concrete shattered his mood. It also jangled plates, cups, and nerves in the boat's interior.

'What the hell was that?' A screech of protest, rather than a question.

'Sorry dear, just nudged a bridge slightly.'

'Look it's quite simple,' the screech now an octave and several decibels lower. 'This strip of water called a canal is what this **canal** boat is supposed to move along. That means we have to go under the bridges, not around them. It's not just the wash that damages canal banks, it's hitting the things! We'll lose our deposit if you put any more dents in my tranquillity.'

'Yes dear. How's the tea coming along?'

'I'll be right up with it as soon as I've found some cups you haven't smashed.' The voice from the boat's kitchen – or galley, as the boaties like to call it – was now a mere rasp, which was a pleasant contrast to the screech.

'Another bridge coming up, dear. I'll see how fast I can take this one.'

'Did you say *'take'* or *'break'*?'

Another clang, this time on the roof.

'Can't you steer this damn thing without demolishing the entire canal? Talk about a hazard to navigation!'

'That wasn't me, dear. There's a man on the roof. He jumped off the bridge.'

'Well, that was rubbish timing. We're the only boat moving at this hour, and he decides to jump into the canal when we're underneath. With luck like that, I'm not surprised he wants to end it all.'

Another clang. Another boarder.

'What is this? Suicide alley, or something? Tell them all to jump off !'

'They've got guns, dear'

'Well, if they've each got a gun, why do they want to do themselves in by jumping off a bridge?'

'I think it's us they want to do in, dear. The guns are pointing at me!'

'Well, if they're some of those damn Somali pirates, the Leeds and Liverpool Canal is a serious miscalculation.'

'I don't think they're pirates. Not an eye patch between them, and a full complement of legs.'

'Well, if it's just because we're late back to the boat-hire base it's rather heavy-handed.'

Two evil-looking characters in black overalls, one wearing a black balaclava, the other a bright orange hoodie, motioned at Roger with the barrels of sub-machine guns.

'You! Listen! We are taking over this boat! Turn it around. We go back to Liverpool.' Snapped Black Balaclava.

'Turn around?' This boat is sixty feet long! How do you suggest I turn it round in a canal only thirty feet wide?'

'You don't argue with the Wirral People's Front!' Orange Hoodie, much shorter and fatter than Black Balaclava, raised his weapon threateningly. 'Turn this ship around, or we shoot you and all your crew!'

'OK, if you're so good at helming one of these things,' Roger smirked inwardly at his use of the boaties' language, 'you take over. No need to shoot. Oh, and it's due back at the hire base by midday. Yesterday. Bye!'

With that, he prepared to jump for the towpath.

'Stop!' It was Black Balaclava. He stood alongside Orange Hoodie on top the boat, both brandishing lethal weaponry, the Laurel and Hardy of the terrorist world. 'The canal widens soon. You turn this boat around when we get there.'

'We boaties call it a winding hole' Another private smirk. 'That's the only way I know to turn, without a crane.'

Two unexpected clangs on the roof, followed by scrabbling sounds and a hefty double splash.

'What was that?' the call from the galley slave below decks.

'Oh, just another bridge. It seems the Wirral People's Front have taken a swimming lesson.'

'Good timing. Tea's ready.'

Lost in the Wilderness

by Anne Sheppard

This poem followed a prompt to write something in the style of the Romantic Poets.

Lost in the wilderness – marooned in the blanket dark,
Where dreams entwine and shadows chase,
As snapshot cameos race through, and memory half wakes
To gather now, where thoughts and fantasies combine
With wispy tendrils, fronds of sleep,
And promises of dreams to keep.

'til morning fair upon the rise of dawn creeps through
To lighten now my room with strands of perfect light,
As threads of dreams are loosed from echoes of the night
And consciousness reflects upon the waiting world beyond,
Where songs of birds intrude and merge in semi dark -
The purest of them all the pirouetting lark.

‘Nostre Dame – Anno Domini Nostri MCLXIX’
From Aquitaine to France
by Alan Jackson

This piece was written in Writing Group after being challenged to write a story inspired by a hobby. One of mine is mediaeval music, and Nostre is the result. Incidentally Leo is a real historical person, but almost nothing is known of his life.

I hate the French. I hate their city, I hate their weather, and especially I hate their King – an arrogant two-faced prig who thinks that because he’s grown a few hairs on his chin he’s better than everyone else in the whole country.

Mind, in France that wouldn’t be difficult.

I admit that when my Leo first floated the idea of moving to France I was quite enthusiastic – well, I could see that my Leo saw it as his big chance, and that would have been enough in itself; but also, it meant I moved out of reach of my parents – oh, don’t get me wrong; I love my parents dearly; but… they say absence makes the heart grow fonder? Especially as they never really approved of Leo, and anyway they are typical Aquitanians – a bit narrow minded. You know the tale of the Aquitanian who went to confession because he’d let his bull mount his cows on a Sunday? They would have sympathised.

So, there we were in Paris, me and my Leo and little Peter, and because Leo, as Succentorelect, was ranked as a Canon of the Cathedral (insofar as it existed) we were allotted a lodging in the Cathedral Close – that is, in the smelliest part of Paris right next to the building site of the new cathedral. Well, at least we got service from the Cathedral, so I didn't need to hire any more servants, and we had room enough for us all – even Martina had a tiny room up in the roof – a servant with her own room! Interesting, though, when you think about it: we were automatically given lodgings big enough for Leo and a wife and children and a maidservant, when my Leo is in minor orders and therefore officially celibate.

It would never have happened in Aquitaine.

Anyway, the first day was spent unpacking and finding the refectory and trying to calm little Peter down and talking to the chamberlain and telling the archbishop's people that we'd arrived and generally getting settled in. It was the second day that my Leo went off to find his choristers while little Peter and I went off exploring the markets and looking round what there was of the new cathedral – and believe me, it is huge. There's only the chancel so far, but that alone is far bigger than any church I've ever seen – far bigger even than the Viscount's great hall in Limoges. We walked all round it on our way to the refectory for lunch, where I tried to talk to some of the other women there.

At that point I discovered another thing I hate about the French. I hate their patois.

After Vespers we got back to our lodgings, put little Peter to bed and settled down to doze in front of the fire and wait for my Leo. I didn't have long to wait – but his kiss woke me up.

'Sweet!' I exclaimed. 'What's wrong?'

He shrugged.

'No, tell me! Have you met the choir? Are they useless? Was it the Precentor? Or the Dean? Are they trying to block your appointment? Tell me!'

He shrugged again and gave me another – very half-hearted – kiss. 'No, nothing like that,' he said. 'It's the building. The new cathedral. You can't hear the neumes.'

Presumably I looked puzzled.

'It's so big, so echoey, the music just smears out. You can hear the individual notes, in fact you can still hear them well after you've stopped singing them, but you can't hear how they fit together – you can't hear the structure, the melody, the rhythm, the movement – you can't hear the neumes.'

This wasn't something I could really help with except by listening – at least till we got to bed.

'And no, the choir aren't co-operating – I wanted to try a few things to see if they made it any better, but they just said that wasn't how you should sing. The Precentor wouldn't listen to me, either.'

I couldn't help with the music, and I probably couldn't help with the choir; but I could at least have a go with the Precentor. He may not want to pay attention to a Limousin cantor, but by Santa Valeria he'll listen to the daughter of an Angevin Sieur whose forebears were lords when Paris was a gaggle of mud huts!

So next morning, after a successful but not totally satisfying night, I passed little Peter on to Martina and went with my Leo into the great new chancel. My footsteps crunched on the mason's dust as I walked a decorous step behind Leo over to the north side where the choir were waiting.

'Who's that?' I whispered.

'Which one?' whispered Leo back.

'The one with a frown on his face that would curdle milk.'

'That's the Precentor, Brother Dionysius! Ssh!'

The Precentor jerked round as my Leo walked up, flicking the tail of his sleeve into the face of another, younger Benedictine a pace or so behind him – presumably his clerk. That meant the Precentor saw me: he reared up to his full height and snorted at my Leo.

'Why have you brought your whore with you when you perform your sacred duties?' he snapped.

'Why not?' I said, 'You've brought yours!'

I really thought he was going to hit me. Instead, he snapped round to glance at his frozen clerk, then spun right round, turning his back on me, my Leo and the choristers, and swept out. His genuflection to the temporary altar was an obvious afterthought. As he went, his clerk glanced at me with a look of pure loathing, opened his mouth as if to say something, then toddled out after his boss.

The choir seemed somewhat cowed by these events; at least they showed no open signs of rebellion like Leo had described. But I could certainly hear the problem: that huge high roof, those thin distant walls, they mixed the notes together so much that the neumes, the structures, just couldn't register. It was just a great squodge of sound, muddy, smudged, cold, ugly, and shapeless.

Just like Paris.

I hung around for a bit, then wandered off to do some shopping, which took me nicely to lunchtime.

The refectory was stone-dusty and noisy and hot and smelly, as you'd expect, but also crowded almost to capacity. I'd hoped for a chance to make friends with some of the other women around, but the best I could do was to perch on one corner of a bench by a gaggle of clerics – more Benedictines. They ignored me, which was a plus after the morning.

After a couple of minutes, the one next to me stood up to go, and another quickly grabbed his place – he'd actually sat down before either of us recognised each other: it was the Precentor's clerk.

'*Tu*!' he hissed in that patois of theirs. '*La dame si cruelle! Por quoi* –' He pulled himself together, mopped up the gruel he'd spilt and started again in proper Latin. 'How could you! How could you be so cruel to me! What had I done! I'd never met you – didn't even know you existed! Why – tell me why you were so cruel!'

The sheer hatred in his words took me aback for a moment. I'd insulted him, yes, and quite strongly, but this venom?

'To destroy in one word all my hopes – all I ever dream of! How could you – and how could you know!'

I suddenly realised what was going on. 'You mean,' I said, 'You're not his – his delight, but you desperately want to be? I didn't know! Truly! I swear, by Our Lady and Saint Martial and Saint Valerie I swear I never even guessed!' My heart was pounding through a mishmash of guilt, shock, and Aquitanian propriety. I would never ever have had a conversation like this even in Limoges, let alone in earshot of my parents – and now I was talking of such things to a man! A strange man!

'I wouldn't've needed that. I only wanted him to notice me – to treat me as a friend. That would have been enough. Just for him to call me Pérotin and me to call him Dionin, I didn't need more. I dreamed of more, of course I did, but it would've been enough. And now you've – you – just in one word, all my hopes, all I'd ever hoped.' Tears were trickling down his face, but in that dust half the men had tears dripping down anyway.

I was sitting in a Paris refectory, but mentally I was in Aquitaine. I knew what I ought to say – I knew what any well-brought-up Aquitanian lady would say – or gentleman for that matter. But I remembered my parents saying it to me when I first began with my Leo, before I'd even spoken to him, just going to listen to his singing in the Abbey.

I remembered how much it hurt me then, and the memory hurt me now. I couldn't say it. The words would not come out.

But I didn't know what I should say. I didn't know what to do. I could hear his words, hear his pain, but it was all so confused, so muddy, smudged, cold, ugly, and shapeless – I could hear the notes, but I couldn't hear the neumes.

With one hand I ate my gruel, with the other I touched my

rosary through the cloth of my pocket. What would Mother Mary have done? She went with the Christ-child from Bethlehem to Egypt. Could I imitate her? Could I go from Aquitaine to France with my Leo, in spirit as well as in body?

The little silence between us stretched and stretched and stretched.

I suddenly remembered Brother Dionysius turning to glance at his clerk when I'd said what I said. I had seen it with my head's Aquitanian eyes – now I saw it with my mind's French eyes. Maybe the Blessed Mother had opened them for me? Maybe she had brought me from Aquitaine to France at last?

I didn't matter. What mattered was that now my way was no longer muddy; it was clear and pure. And it left me with no choice at all.

'Brother Dionysius is a priest here, as well as at your abbey?'

He jumped. 'Er yes, yes of course.'

'So, he hears confessions here? Where? When?'

'Third bay on the north side. The hour before nones. But please –' His face was a mask of horror.

'Oh, I will say nothing of this. But I have sinned, and I must be shriven.' I paused. 'I swear to say nothing to anyone else but – I should tell my Leo what happened. He can be trusted to keep silent, and he is my man.'

'They say Aquitanians are…'

'Tight about such matters, and about their women talking to strangers. Yes. Not as bad as the Tolosans, they don't approve even of married couples kissing. And we once had a visitor from Albi, and he wouldn't speak to any married woman – not even to my mother who was his hostess – because they had 'debased the purity of their spirit with the contamination of the material world.' But yes. Leo ought to know what I've been doing.'

Brother Dionysius was struck dumb when I presented myself to be shriven by him, but his vows held – he could not refuse. Obviously I'm not going to tell you what I said in Confession, but I did keep my promise – not even the slightest suggestion that I had said anything to anyone. All I did was to drop in the assumption that he would be going to – or maybe already had – spoken to his clerk about the incident. I didn't even let on I knew his clerk's name.

Leo wasn't quite as grey as he'd been the last night. We split a tasson of ale between us, and he perked up quite a bit – I think it might've been the dust as much as anything else. He perked up a lot more when I told him about my lunch; in fact, he laughed so much ale came out of his nose.

So next morning once again my Leo and I walked into the great new chancel. This time we'd got in before Brother Dionysius; but Leo was still chalking the music out on the staveboard when he arrived. And this time with a smile on his face that lit up the whole chancel, and with his clerk equally beaming, a pace or so in front.

'Now as I said yesterday!' My Leo was haranguing the choir. 'Try! Stre-etch to the next neume and hit its first note clean and hard!'

'It's not how we do it in France!' muttered one of the choristers – an oldish man. 'We do the opposite! We have always done the opposite! What you are saying is not French; it is –'

'What he is saying is right!' Brother Dionysius cut in. 'Why would we bring in a new succentor all the way from Saint Martial if the French way of singing worked in here? Now I want to hear you doing exactly what he tells you to, I want to see you paying proper respect to him and to this his good woman, or else you can give up your nice comfortable office here and go back to your parishes and live again on the pittance they will pay you. Excuse me, Brother Succentor, I interrupted you; please carry on.'

'Nothing to excuse, Brother Precentor.' My Leo turned to the choir. 'So Stre-etch and hit!'

'How much do we stretch it by?' The face was sulky but accepting the inevitable.

'Oh, a long way – maybe even double or – yes, go for double. Got it? Last note of each neume stretched to double length and the first note hit. Sing!'

But I was looking at the clerk. He was smiling almost round his head: he stepped sideways out of the others' eyelines and whispered to me.

'*Nos – nos avons – jo sui Perotin a son Dionin! Par Nostre Dame et Saint Rémi, jo sui tousjours* – I am for ever in your debt, beloved Lady. For ever in the ages of ages!'

I smiled back, remembering – remembering when I first kissed my Leo. But that was back in Aquitaine, and now I was in France, truly in France, with my Leo and his music that were lifting me far above memories to the reality of now: music no longer muddy but music that was clear and pure.

I looked at my Leo; I listened to the music.

And I could hear the neumes.

Turning Turtle
by Ann Revill

This piece was written in response to an exercise to tell a story without a main character.

The yacht rocked in the slight swell. The sea, blue as lapis lazuli, retained no hint of threat or disaster. The tropical storm had passed as if it had never been. Out of a cloudless sky a gull appeared and landed flat-footed on the foredeck. Preening itself for a minute or two, it cocked its head as if listening for signs of life. Alone in the silence, it gave a harsh cry, shook its tail feathers, and then took off in search of fish.

The halyards slapped lazily at the masthead, the only sound now, apart from the soft wash from the bow, hitting the ripples on the surface of the ocean. From the stern trailed a frayed cable, swinging aimlessly to and fro in the yacht's wake, whatever it once held lost during the night.

A tangle of ropes and canvas cluttered the deck and the cabin door hung slack in the well, its lock smashed, boards splintered: below, sea water slopped in the companionway. Two bunks spilled their sodden blankets into the salt pool, where galley pans bobbed alongside the waterlogged charts. The lantern, extinguished in the capsize, hung at a drunken angle, its glass shattered.

The tattered remnants of sails shivered. A slight breeze

stirred the surface, and the boat began to move gently eastward, dipping to the waves. A dolphin surfaced close to the stern and soon there were half a dozen, escorting the crippled yacht on its solitary journey. Curved backs rose smoothly from the sea and slid noiselessly back underwater. For a couple of miles they kept vigil by the boat and then disappeared as silently as they had come.

The breeze drove the yacht into the path of a current and it picked up speed. Soon it was moving towards a group of islands on the horizon. The water in the cabin sloshed and churned. A sudden flurry of sparks from the ship's radio fizzed by the chart table.

A disembodied voice jerked, 'Control to *Albatross*. What is your position? Repeat, what is your position?'

A few crackles, a flash, and the radio went dead. The last human sound. The wind dropped as the boat neared the islands and she began drifting again. Soft bumps on her hull jolted her along, out of the mainstream of the current and towards the nearest atoll. Around her sides the ungainly shapes of turtles flailed towards the shore, a vast regiment of armoured sea creatures, following the driving instinct which led them each year to this island, this season. Nearing the shore, they abandoned their companion and made for the shelving beach. The yacht bobbed on the waves, edging closer until she grounded on the white sand, listing gradually until she lay on her side.

The turtles, about their business, ignored her. They were scraping holes in the sand and one by one began to lay their rubbery eggs. By nightfall, task completed, they had returned to the ocean, leaving the sun to incubate the offspring they would never see.

Only the boat remained. Following high tides carried her further up the deserted beach and left her to decay and silt up.

The eggs hatched and those young which escaped the sharp beaks of marauding sea birds, scrambled down to the protective waters of the ocean. When they matured, they too would come back to the same shore. As the yacht sank further into the sand each year, some turtles would even scoop a hole in its well and drop their soft eggs into its warmth, covering them with strong strokes of their flippers.

The Seven Consolations of Spring
by Anna Quartly

Inspired by Anna's love of walking in the Cotswold countryside

---

The first consolation of spring
are the spooned-petals
of Magnolia cups.
Her vanilla palms
encircle nectar-filled buds of sweeping sunlight –
embracing the watercolour sky.

The second consolation,
the slow beat
of a Monarch's wing.
Unfanning her blackened cloak,
she flutters through smokeless air, colouring your eyes,
lands on your finger with hair-thin legs.

And the third consolation,
the sugary flesh
of Pomegranate fruit.
Ruby gems burst –
jewels, like sweet liqueur stick to your teeth –
embracing the watercolour sky.

And the fourth consolation,
the globed moons
of Wren's eggs.
Mottled in cinnamon freckles,
they're tucked away under a treasure chest of twigs and leaves.
Unhatched.

And the fifth consolation
is the sun's yoke
dripping into the milky clouds.
Light swims and turns,
transforms into a thick river of treacle, nourishing the frail.
embracing the watercolour sky.

And the sixth consolation,
the scurry
of a Squirrel's tail,
hops and hooks its claws
with scoffed cheeks on Cedar bare branches
in the simmering heat.

And the seventh consolation,
the crunch of footsteps,
hardened in soil.
The cold shifts –
into a warm coat of wind, nursing the young.
Embracing the watercolour sky.

Jellyfish
by Anna Quartly

---

puffed smoke, hushed souls,
boneless gums and brainless heads,
translucent blood.
silked membranes – ribbon-like, coiled
temptation, looped venom.
Pulsing Blooms.

cloudless

The Phone Bill
by Jane Gray-Wallis

It wasn't so very long ago that folk did not have a phone in their pocket. Phones were in a red box at the corner of the street. Somewhere you would probably find a defibrillator, or a book swap these days. Some folk had one in the house. It was plugged in to the wall in the hallway. Somewhere cold and public. Just as well because the cost of using it was a constant worry.

I don't think our Da's got the hang of the phone. He's never been one fur cuddling up, you know, like tucking it under yer chin. He just won't do it. He's been that way since Cousin Nelly rang up to say that Uncle Jack had been knocked down by the bank manager. He said he never saw 'im coming, Uncle Jack that is.

When the phone rings I go and sit on the stairs. You can hear everything that goes on from the top of our stairs. And, if you push your head through the gap in the bars you can look right down to the table with the phone on. There it goes 'dring, dring.' I hear the front room door open and Da calling 'Mother the phone's ringing.' I hear the muffled voice of mi Mam from the kitchen. Then I see mi Da, at least I see the top of his head. He approaches cautious, like a lion stalking its prey. He looks over his shoulder to see if help is coming and then, just as you might imagine it'll stop ringing, he jumps forward and grabs it. Once in his hand he keeps a steady grip on the receiver, lest it should run away I suppose. Then, holding it at approximately arm's length he shouts, 'Hello ....Hello .... Hello.' This is mi Mam's cue for her entrance. 'Oh, give it here.' She snatches the phone from mi Da and clearing her throat she brings out her telephone voice. 'Hello… can I help?' I see her frown. 'Alright, I'll tell him.' Then, shoving the phone back at mi Da, she says 'It's only Arthur wanting to know if you'll be playing in the match this Sunday.' And she stamps back off to the kitchen. I see mi Da carefully replace the receiver. Then he sighs and says to himself 'no need to phone, he could have asked me at the Dog tonight.' Then he goes back into the front room closing the door ever so gently like a man trying not to wake a sleeping baby.

Our Emma's a right one with the phone. She comes home from school and rings her friend Sal straight away. I have to do mi homework, and feed mi rabbit, and set the table, and put out the napkins, and put the plates on the table. All the while Mam's saying 'can you do this please Emma?' While Emma just shouts 'I'm on the phone.' Even when the doorbell rings, I have to squeeze by while she shouts 'Somebody … I'm on the phone!' If it's mi friend Tracy, she rolls her eyes and says 'she's on the phone.' Then we go upstairs to play. There's nothing interesting about Emma's phone calls it's just a lot of, 'he said to her ….. an she said to him.' Not that Sal doesn't know all this cos she only left Emma at the bus stop ten minutes before. Honestly!

It's a bit more interesting sometimes. Sometimes she gets a call after tea. It's the only time mi Da tries to answer the phone. He nips out the front room but he's no match for her bounding out of the kitchen. She scoops up the phone and says 'hello,' all puffed out as if she's been running even though she's only come out of the kitchen. Then, off she goes moving this way an that twisting the cord between her fingers and smiling – all the while. Anyway, Da's in the kitchen bi now. 'She's murmuring' he'll say, 'she's murmuring.' I hear his voice getting louder, finally he'll open the kitchen door, sudden like, an say 'don't forget who's payin the bill.'

It's not a good idea to ask fer more pocket money when the phone bill comes. Sam, mi brother, says it's a day when inflation takes over so best to keep a low profile. Da gets inflated alright. I see 'im through the crack in the kitchen door. His vest is so tightly stretched you'd think it would split. His face is red, he's bellowing and whacking the phone bill as if he would like to punch it to oblivion. Ma says nowt but keeps on cooking, moving about between sink and oven and shooing Da out the way wi flaps of her tea towel. It's only when he gets to the end of the speech that she'll say, 'Give over Joe.' Once his bellowing dies down to a whisper Mam pats him on the shoulder and goes to the dresser to fetch out her tin. 'Here you are Joe, I've got a bit put by.'

I love Mam's tin. It often saves the day.

My Kathleen Doesn't Shout

by Tim Melling

I wrote this story as a reflection on the wider impact of Alzheimer's and dealing with loss – something I have witnessed in my own family.

'Here look at this' David called. 'I found it in the Reader's Digest Guide to the British Isles.'

My brother and I were clearing out the bungalow. He handed me a piece of writing paper, Basildon Bond, smooth to the touch. I recognised Mum's immaculate flowing hand-writing. She had headed it 'My Kathleen doesn't Shout' and it began, 'Tonight was one of the bleaker nights. She checked the catheter, it was working. Knitting was out, her hands were too painful. She listened to the radio with the sound low so as not to disturb him. No-one called...' The 'she' was Mum, writing about herself in the third person.

Mum had died three weeks before. It was unexpected. My father, ravaged by Alzheimer's, survived her for three weeks. He died on New Year's Eve. That was not the plan. My hope for her was that Dad would die sooner or later and Mum would have her life back, at least for a few years.

'No-one called..' That struck home like a spear in my chest. I'd phone her most Saturdays to compare notes over the Telegraph crossword. I'd ask her how she was.

'We're fine' she would always say. We're fine – never 'I'm

fine' It was as if she had merged their two existences into one. She never liked to 'bother us.' Saw her role as looking after rather than being looked after. 'My Kathleen doesn't shout.'

'No-one called.' I should have known; I should have visited more often. But I consoled myself, I have a job and a young family. I felt anger rising in my throat towards Dad as if he had stolen her life. She existed only for him.

When Dad died, I felt relief. They say that with Alzheimer's you grieve twice. Once when they get it and start to fade, the second time when they die. I grieved once, but that once lasted years.

After Mum's death, we moved Dad into a nursing home. We visited him every day.. A receptionist was reading a magazine when we arrived. She nodded us through to the living area where the resident's watched TV or chatted. Dad sat in a wheelchair facing the TV. He had a red blanket over his lap. He recognised me.

'Hello Dad.'

He made a noise, a sound like a caterwaul of anguish. I don't know that it was anguish though. Debbie, my wife, asked him if he enjoyed it here.

'No!' he said with surprising passion and force. Then he stared at his blanket making noises to himself. We were taken with him up to his room. It was warm. There was a hospital bed: tubes, levers, and pulleys so they could lift him to wash and change him.

On the window ledge some flowers were arranged in a bowl. By the opposite wall stood a simple dresser and a photo I recognised. It had been taken in 1982 when he was Mayor. It was at the Mayoral Gala. It showed Mum in a sage green top wearing the Lady Mayor's chain. She was looking at the camera, laughing. Dad was sitting on her right in his mayoral regalia saying something to her, maybe a joke. He was smiling. He liked to tell jokes. When he lay in bed, he would be able to see that picture. I wondered if he missed her.

We left when it got dark.

A few days before he died, Debbie visited him. As she sat by the bed, she felt Mum's presence there as a source of warmth and happiness. She saw Dad look across over her shoulder and his face shone with recognition and happiness. It was a nice thought. I cried when she told me.

Mum was always Dad's champion. She carried the torch for him. She saw something in him, a commitment to making the world a better place maybe. She described how they first met, at a teacher training college in Cheshire, where she noticed that when speaking, he had a habit of covering his mouth with his hand and a slight stammer. When he came back after the war, she described him as fractured, delicate, as if he might shatter at any moment.

Throughout their life together, they were both active in local politics and the community. Our house was used as a base during election campaigns. Meetings were held in our dining room in the evening. When we were little, David and I used to sit at the top of the stairs listening – before we were discovered and packed off to bed. I remember the noise of debate, the sound of laughter and the smell of cigarettes wafting up from the dining room. We spent many evenings listening to the fun.

In our house we had a walk-in cupboard under the stairs. In it were the electricity and gas meters, shelves stacked with boxes of different size nails and screws, coats and jackets. To my child's eyes the cupboard spoke of undiscovered treasure. At the very back of the cupboard, near where the stairs meet the floor (I had to worm my way through the bags and boxes to get there) was an old leather-bound suitcase. On it were exotic and colourful stickers. Inside were an old brown leather flying helmet with shiny Bakelite earpieces that stuck out of the side, goggles and a green rubber oxygen mask that attached to the helmet. The mask had a microphone piece built in and an oxygen tube attached. The case also contained a pair of black, silk and fur lined suede leather flying boots (my Dad told me that they were meant to be shrapnel proof) and a small silk flag bearing the words 'Don't shoot I am English' in Russian and the Union Jack.

I used to wear this gear when sledging down the bull field in the snow. Dad would come with us and one year broke his nose on landing after a jump. That would not have happened had he been wearing his flying mask. He was happy for me to wear it though.

He only ever talked about his war experience once. We were on a walking tour of the Howgill fells in Cumbria. They are the smooth voluptuous hills east of the Lake District. It was evening; we were drinking beer. Dad talked about his life in the RAF during the war. He was the navigator and bomb aimer in a Mosquito fighter bomber. His squadron was based in Norfolk. That explained summer holidays exploring Norfolk towns and villages and Dad staring wistfully over gates into what looked like wheat fields, but I now realised were his old flying bases.

In Europe he flew missions over Normandy, Belgium, and Germany. He holds the record for the lowest bail out from a damaged plane. It shattered his knees, and he spent 6 months recovering in hospital in Hoylake. I don't remember much more that he said, too much beer! I picked up fragments after his death from family, and old documents and letters. The plane he bailed out of was hit over Normandy. His Pilot, Charlie, managed to get back over the channel and told Dad to 'get out.' Charlie perished in the crash. Dad wrote to his parents – we have their reply thanking him for his kind words about their son. He was a good man was Dad.

I still have his logbook and training manual, full of his beautiful copper plate handwriting and engineer precise drawings. He returned to the air in early '45 and saw action over Belgium and Germany. He was demobbed in 1946, qualified as a teacher a career he relished, retiring from teaching in 1982.

It's 1985, Dad has just been heckled down at a County Council meeting. Mum, a county councillor stands up and defends him with surprising ferocity. She is normally very calm. Fred had lost his words, and tried to find them, but what came out of his mouth made no sense. The opposition cruelly jeered him. He got flustered and sat down, agitated. Kath stood and shamed them. It was most unlike her, normally so calm and warm. She was like ice. 'My Kathleen doesn't shout. 'People could not look at her. She came down to Fred and left the chamber with him.'

'Lost his words.' That is what Paul said about his Grandpa when he and Granny came to visit. This was before any of us would admit to ourselves or anyone else that something was wrong. 'He's always been a bit absent minded' we would say. We would play Trivial Pursuit together and be relieved when he remembered something. Everything would be alright. We were living in Hertfordshire; one night I took Dad to the Bull, a local friendly pub, nothing fancy, just good beer. We sat in a corner and chatted. I noticed that Dad would keep repeating himself. 'So, are you enjoying yourself down here, Tom?' He would ask. I would answer, then 5 minutes later the same question again. Eventually I reminded him, 'Dad you've already asked me that question.'

He stared at the table and with quiet, ferocious intensity, and said slowly, 'You do not know what this is like.' Then he continued as if nothing had happened and still repeated his questions.

He was right, but I was terrified.

Shortly after, some friends came to visit. Paul was 2 years old. It was Spring and the bluebells were out. Walking was a joy; you could feel the earth uncoiling after winter and the sun was warm on our backs. Paul was on my shoulders. At one point I shouted, 'where's Paul?' He pulled my hair and said, 'here silly' and laughed. I didn't.

Alzheimer's is called 'The thief in the night' It creeps in and steals your faculties in reverse order. Although Dad had moments of lucidity, he lost his short-term memory, he lost his sentences, he lost his words. Towards the end I remember him walking restlessly around his tiny bungalow going 'ga-ga-ga-ga-ga-ga' like a machine gun.

The day I finally accepted Dad had the disease, I was at home. Debbie said, 'he is not going to get better.' I felt a rush of grief bubble up through me and explode out of my mouth. It was the first time I had cried for years. Now I will never know my Dad. Who do I turn to when I need help? I am losing him, but he is still here, to remind me now, here, of what I have lost. I will get glimpses, but even when he tries it's as if the effort exhausts him and his words run into the sand.

Mum gets more noble by the week. She makes the sacrifice. 'We are fine. He had a good night.'

'How are you Mum?'

'Would you like a cup of tea and some biscuits? Maybe a sandwich?'

'Why don't you come and visit?'

'Yes' meaning, change the subject. 'My Kathleen doesn't shout.'

The one time she did visit, Dad escaped from the secure home where he was staying and was found wandering along a road in the dark 5 miles away by the police. Mum went straight back. That was the last time she left him.

Shortly before she died, I went to visit Mum. It was October, the sun still had some warmth and the trees in the garden still had colour. We walked around the garden.

'That dogwood came from Harlow Carr. Freddy planted it when we moved here.'

I went to the shed with her. We could hear the school

children playing on the other side of the fence. She liked that. It soothed her, continuity, happiness. She used to be a teacher. In the shed I found an easel and drawings that Dad had made.

'He liked to draw, it seemed to ease him.'

'Maybe when words fail you, you can still speak though drawing.' I said.

On the way back into the house she stopped suddenly and said. 'You know I love you all, don't you?'

'Yes mum. Of course, we do.' I wondered why she was telling me this now. I didn't ask.

'I want you to know that I am content' she said. 'I don't mind what happens. You, David, and James will be alright.'

'Yes Mum.' my heart was beating quicker, my mouth was dry. I could not ask the question.

But on 4th December 1998 at 11.47am, sitting amongst the catheters, the tubes, and the bottles, holding her still warm hand, grief and regret overwhelmed me.

The Hiraeth
by Caroline Bennett

Move to a shining foreign city,
Explore some modern marvel,
As you float back to your apartments,
You will spot a poky embassy museum.
Step inside.

Exhibit One: On a pedestal, behind a retractable barrier,
A Friday night walk home from school through the splashy dark,
Lamb chop fat crisping under the grill,
An empty ice cream carton folded flat for cats.

Exhibit Two: Crammed inside a dusty cabinet,
A Brecon Beacon pocked by hail,
A queue for boiled seaweed,
A Morris man with a can of bitter.

Exhibit Three: In a badly lit basement, with beanbags,
A guided tour of chips and gravy,
An interactive display of Aberavon Shopping Centre, broken,
A dressing up box of lost rugby matches, different sizes.

In the Giftshop:
Your favourite accent on a postcard,
A blanket woven the traditional way, with English infliction and Welsh resistance,
A room spray of Male Voice Choir
A hefted lamb, freshly shorn from the hill.

The Lamp Post
by Alison Jackson

The inspiration for this piece came from a set of words given to us at the meeting.

It's not a very nice view from my window, though it's a nice window. A lovely bay with my chair and a table. There's the remote for the television, but there's only so much TV you can watch. I do have some lovely carers, but you never quite know when they'll come. Fortunately, I can still get to the bathroom and into the kitchen with my frame, but I can't get dressed on my own any more or cook.

I spend most of the day in my chair and I like to watch what is going on in the street from my window. The houses this side of the road are quite big and have mostly been converted into flats, like this one. Before things got so bad, I was sorry it wasn't on the ground floor – all those stairs – but now I like having a wider view over the top of the hedge.

The houses opposite are smaller, terrace houses with little gardens at the front. I think they must have something at the back as well – perhaps garages, because I often see cars going up the entry opposite my window towards the lamp post where the back lane crosses over.

A lot of life seems to happen by that lamp post. I don't sleep very well, so I get up early and use my Zimmer to get over to my chair. They used to tell me off for it, but I said that it gave me a headache to keep in bed when I was awake, so now they have put a rug by the chair, so I don't get cold. First thing, all the cars come out with people going off to work. When I was young, it would have been men, but it's just as likely to be the women now. Most of them know I'm there and wave before turning into the street. I've never spoken to any of them, but it's friendly. I tell myself they're asking if I slept well and how I am feeling this morning.

A bit later, it's the children running past the lamp post off to school. It's a bit of a short cut to use the back alley rather than the road. The early ones come along chatting and then just before 9, they're all running. I used to love running when I was their age.

After that it's the dog walkers. I counted the other day – 23 dogs sniffed at that lamp post and the males all marked it. Sometimes at night, I see a fox doing the same thing in the light of the lamp. The next morning the dog walkers really struggle to get their animals past it; I smile to think that they don't know why.

Then there's a lull until the children get back from school and the cars back from work. There are some good programmes on daytime TV, and of course they come and give me lunch and they come and help me undress and put me to bed – just as if I were a little child. It's far too early, of course, but I understand that they don't get paid to work late, so when they've gone, I just get up again and go and sit in my chair until I'm sleepy. Sometimes I'm still there in the morning, but they don't know that.

I like watching the lamp post in the evenings. There was a young couple used to meet there; they'd kiss passionately – I remember feeling like that 65 years ago. Then one night, she waited for nearly an hour and when he finally turned up, it was clear that they had a blazing row and I never saw them again; I'm sorry about that.

Recently, though, I've been a bit worried. After dark, there's a man who comes and stands under the lamp post with a rucksack. He stays there for about an hour and lots of other people come to meet him. He seems to be selling something from his rucksack and I think it may be drugs. I couldn't think why he would choose somewhere where I could see him, and then I realised that I don't have my light on when I get up again; it's a bit silly – of course the carers wouldn't come and check-up – but it's nice sitting in the dark looking out.

Anyway, this man under the lamp post. I know that the young people today think of drugs like we used to think of cigarettes and alcohol, and I don't want to interfere or be a killjoy. But some of these kids look very young, and the older ones look desperate. So, a few days ago, I rang the police station. She was very polite, but I think she thought I was just a fussy old woman. Even so, a couple of nights later, a courting couple came along the road – and it really isn't a romantic road. Anyway, they stopped by the alley and started kissing. The man was there – he looked to see whether they wanted anything, but they were too tied up in each other and he ignored them. After a few minutes, they broke apart and went on down the road with their arms round each other. But before they moved on, he looked at my window and smiled.

And the very next night the police came. I only saw the one car which went up the alley from our street, but there must have been others in the back lane, because the man and the two people with him tried to run but I saw him brought back with handcuffs on and put in the car. What a commotion, with blue lights and sirens and all the neighbours putting their lights on and looking out.

And then this morning, two very nice policemen called. I have a camera and can buzz the door open, so I let them in, and they made us all a cup of tea. It was so nice to have fresh tea instead of from a thermos. It was lovely to have visitors and a nice chat. I'll keep an eye on that lamp post, but I hope I only see nice things in future.

The fox was there again just now.

A Classification of Dragonfire
by Nastasya (Tia) Parker

Worship

In the beginning we were angels. Mercenaries, trained to defend and adore. I disregarded that an eternity ago, although my memory has been recently refreshed.

Is it any wonder we hoard treasure? We come from a shimmering, pre-world world beyond Pearly Gates, our pre-time time spent praising the pre-Creation Creator.[1] Awed flames itched our throats; bland, blond, blind, in humbly cowering tongues, whipped to soft peaks.

Envy

Soon after this orb's inception, her Parents disputed what she should be when she grew up. We saw she was being given to humans; our Master coveted your worship more than ours.

In battle, my kind broke from the other angels, seeking the free will you'd snatched for yourselves. We turned our fire against our previous allies, fire quick and fickle, leaping with faith in our own worth, carelessly extinguished.

---

[1] *In this regard we shared purpose with princesses, our longtime prey. Often, they were kept secluded, with pining as their sole occupation, practicing reverence-steeped curtseys for their fathers.*

Rage

So we were banished, to the infant planet's roiling core. We faced that agony, and swallowed it. Once you've gulped torment, you can spit rage.

Eventually, the humans unleashed upon the earth became harmful. So the planet released us, with the blaze we'd percolated in our bellies for millennia. A weighty blaze, rumbling red, spewing swirling spheres.

Hunger

Known for voraciousness, we weren't intended to be eaters. But we'd envied humans' ability to indulge appetites, to recognise hunger in the first place.[2]

When dragons swooped from the depths, we feasted on armies, vanquishing them with ravenous breaths. Breaths of stale, starved smoke wreathing dark, menacing flames, teased into a desperate dance.

Passion

After centuries of unmitigated devouring, we noticed your fairer sex.

Recognising worship as a precarious base for a relationship, instead we were domineering, leaving no room for that free will you'd all been given, obliterating protest with our passionate heat. Heat curling our talons, ejecting in long, luminous, uncontrollable streams.

Disappointment

In the Dark Ages your forebears decided progress hadn't

---

2 *Recently opened cross-party dialogue has revealed to me that not all humans have been granted equal opportunities for indulgence, or even for satiation. This imbalance will be remedied forthwith.*

been worth it and attempted to plunge backward.[3] It was a filthy era. We had to consider where we got our meals, so we targeted princesses.

Monarchs appreciated the opportunity to rid themselves of excess females. Knights bribed kings to send rivals after me, and kings siphoned ransoms off my way, to look as if they cared. A heartless and uninspiring system, sticking me with a frightened princess who submitted to me because she had submitted all her life. I was a mere tool yet didn't object because I chiseled gold and girls from the bargain.

My apathy made poor kindling, soppy and wet. Petulant, blue-rimmed flames, souring my throat and prickling my eyes.

Stubbornness

We stopped caring when the earth grumbled about human proliferation. Your treasures changed, from gold to black—the gushing liquid you stole from her, and the gadgets you bonded with.

I passed the time by laying my victims' skeletons atop their old gowns in a grand procession from brocade to satin to sequins. I stacked my coins, aligning their rims.

Every few years I grabbed a princess,[4] roasting her with force of habit. Orange, efficient fire, carefully aimed so as not to upset the decor, leaving a metallic aftertaste.

Frustration

Your turn came. I set you down in my cave and you kicked through my skeletons with your hideous trainers; snatched a

---

[3] *My description of this period is specific to this region; my kin who established themselves further East knew great development at that time.*

[4] *Princesses by this time had been promoted from burdens to ornaments. Their increased visibility made their capture more inconvenient, but their brief company more pleasurable.*

coin in my counting house. 'All this bling. You trying to compensate for something?'

'You're not behaving like a real princess.' Smoke rode my words.

'Like you're the first to notice. I'm not convinced you're a real dragon, if this is what gets your fire going.' You replaced the coin, half a millimetre to the right. Your impudence sent heat plunging to my stomach. 'You're no better than my dad.'

I could have immolated you then, but I thought you deserved worse than a blaze of frustration. It would have been a hasty blaze, jolting out bright not deep, a knot of fumes lingering in the chest.

Curiosity

You pulled a shiny slab from your pocket and pressed it to your ear. 'Hey Dad, got captured by the dragon. Awkward, I know. Soz. Can you send some guys?'[5]

You pocketed the gadget, shook back your unkempt hair, and faced me. 'Right. Are you ready to take down some condescending, gropey princelings?'

Short-lived though human grievances are, your eyes smouldered with pain. A different heat tingled in my middle. I hadn't felt such flickers of engagement in many a century. Prancing flickers, scampering warmth, gold-tipped and glowing, orange-centered and enticing.

Vengeance

Helicopters swarmed. I let you climb on my back and we took off to investigate. Beetle-helmeted soldiers with weapons thrice the size of their arms incinerated a path through the

---

5 *Most rulers could no longer get away with losing a daughter. Some of my kind had resorted to stealthier abductions—one colleague killed a famous princess by disguising the scene as a car wreck.*

trees. Branches writhed like worms and the earth shuddered.

Through ash and smoke, inside a helicopter's open door, we saw a pristine gown waiting. Your rescue would be strictly conditional. You were their hostage, not mine.

The new role of rescuer swelled my breast with righteous inferno, blood-scarlet, pierced by new perspective.

Faith

You tensed around me at the sight of the dress, symbol of narrow expectations.[6] Your trainers left muddy footprints over my hide. 'Light them up.' Your whisper scalded my ear. Conviction united us, so sharp between my wings it was almost cold.

I inhaled deeply, scents of brushed silk and singed bough, military fuel and soldier sweat and your well-worn jeans. Then I released a new flame: white lightning, fast and brash, mad and glad, eviscerating and evaporating.

Comfort

After the battle we fled. Now from cliffsides to forest depths to castle ruins we make camp, you haggling, sometimes snatching food.

My treasures are smooth beech nuts, coloured leaves. I recline on moss and bury my snout in fresh earth while you plot a more widespread liberation.

We sleep by crackling fire, sunrise-rosy and midnight-cosy, so warm that as I drift off I lose sense for which flames I carry inside and which I've brought forth for you.

---

6 *And what had I been doing all my life but blundering between the walls of narrow expectations? See also: Worship*

Run over by a Jitterbug
by Joan Bartholomew

(Jitterbug – Juggernaut: Processional cart for the idol of Vishnu) a piece inspired by Joan's memories of her mother.

Father was silent behind the paper; Mother coming back from shopping removed her gloves, scarf, and hat.

'You'll never guess who I met?'

'Tell me,' I said.

'Well, who should I meet outside the butchers but Mrs. Mays, and do you know what? Poor George has had a stroke only a slight one. He is better now but it was such a shock.'

'Oh dear, when did it happen?'

'She came home from the W.I. on Thursday and found him!'

'Found him?'

'There he was, prostituted on the floor.'

Father lowered the paper.

'Didn't think George had it in him,' Father said.

There was always news when Mother had been shopping. Some new drama, some tragedy just averted.

'Mrs. Jones nearly had a terrible accident. She was crossing over the street just by the Co-op. You know near that sharp bend. I know it is not a good place to cross but she was in a hurry to get the fish she had just bought home to cook for

Tom's tea. He is very partial to a piece of fresh haddock.'

'Yes, yes, Mother, never mind about the haddock. What happened?'

'Well, coming much too fast round the corner came one of those great big jitterbugs. She managed to get on the pavement, but she dropped the fish and Tom had to have beans on toast. Imagine!'

'Imagine!' said Father.

I arrived late one Friday night and Mother fussed.

'I'm glad you telephoned. A breakdown on the cold shoulder! Never mind, you are here now, and I have made one of those palavers your father likes. You know dear, all meringue and fluffy. Now your Aunt Connie she always makes that loose bottomed Belgian tart with all that butter, she says Uncle Fred particularly likes it.'

Father rustled his paper, lowered it and looked at me over the top. He raised an eyebrow.

'Fred was over there during the war,' he said, clearing his throat.

Father and I did not need to go into town to find out what was happening.

'Mrs. Linsell had a new grandson. There were problems you know. Her daughter had to have that F.B.I. treatment to get pregnant. Then when the baby was born they had to put him in an incinerator for a while. He is fine now. She's ever so pleased. She's going to buy him two of those growbags,' Mother reported.

'That should see he doesn't grow up a shrimp like his father,' commented Father. Mother looked slightly bemused.

'You know all that building work that has been going on down the road, down the road at number 14, Mrs. Tillot had such a nice display of pansies. I wonder where she got them, I must ask her, still, they are too pale for me I like the rich dark colours.'

'And the building work?'

'O yes, well it is very nice. All glass on the side of the house. She has always wanted a little conservative on the side.'

'Didn't we all Mother,' I said, 'didn't we all.'

'Mrs. Lovett has got the decorators in,' said Mother, 'She's having the hall and stairs done. All cream in the hall except that bit at the bottom, you know the dildo she is having that done pink.'

'Is she now,' I said.

The next day we hear about the Mother's Union outing. They were going to Blackpool for the hallucinations.

'Now tomorrow I am going to collect a prescription for Mrs. Brown from the chemist, its ointment for inflation of the leg she has.'

Everyone's mother seems to be doing it. Linda told me that her mother had telephoned to say that she was having her hall painted and was putting semtex on the ceiling, to sort out the damp. Linda's husband said, 'Well that gets rid of the damp *and* the mother-in-law problem then.'

It was Linda's mother who had been to the Mother's Union to a talk on North American Indians. 'Ever so interesting, all about Chiefs and their Squawks.'

Mrs. Fawcett's daughter is expecting a baby. 'It's overdue, they are going to take her in on Wednesday and seduce her if it has not come by then.'

'Really,' I said.

'Poor Mrs. Fawcett,' continues Mother, 'she is worried about losing her facilities.'

'That would make life very awkward,' agreed Father.

Sadly, Mrs. Brown's husband is in prison. 'Oh yes,' she said, 'he's been incastrated there for six months. He's working in the library, him being a solicitor, well, the computer it went wrong he had a floppy dick I understand. So annoying for him.'

'This year I bought my cards from the Royal Society for the

Prevention of Birds. Such a good charity,' Mother said.

Then we went to Midnight Mass. It was cold and the town ladies wore their furs. Without her hearing aid Mother spoke loudly, waiting to greet the Vicar.

'Did you see Mrs. Jollicliffe's coat?'

'Um, no Mother,' I replied, checking that Mrs. Jollicliffe was not too near.

'It's not real mink you know dear, only stimulated,' Mother continued.

'I do hope not Mother,' I said.

Father put a handkerchief to his face.

'Happy Christmas, Vicar,' we all said.

Tir na n'Óg

by Alan Jackson

The boring day of work is done
The nightward sky's seagreen
With waves of sunset gold that lap
The isles of Tir na n'Óg
I board the carriage, trampling feet
And bags and coats and pride
A youthful mouth laughs out a phrase
A language of the Elder Days
The tongue of Tir na n'Óg
The chemo's failed, the cancer's won
Cold panic wakes my night
For me the darkness comes, and yet
My sunset, laughing, still awaits
Golden, free, unconquered light
The light of Tir na n'Óg

The Captive's Song
by Alan Jackson

The road I walk I walk alone
The road that all must go.
I walk towards the dark I see
To find the light I know.

The road I walk I walk alone
Destined to walk from birth
I know the moans and weeping pain
But in my heart sleeps mirth.

The road I walk I walk alone
I do not choose to run
I walk the path towards defeat
That shows my victory won.

The Paddling Pool

by Anne Sheppard

This piece was written following a prompt to write a horror story

---

It was hot and Samantha could feel a headache starting. She tied her hair back so that she could see what she was doing.

Christopher had been asking all morning if they could get the paddling pool out and she had finally relented. It was kept in the garage, and she had struggled to pull it down off the racking that Robert had installed the previous year. Now she knelt on the grass trying to work out how the last bit of frame clipped together.

It was the luxury model, or it had been when they had bought it years ago for their two older children. All singing all dancing, with a plywood seat at each corner. The two older children had loved it and so had Christopher last year when aged two he had sat in it for the first time, surrounded by his bath time toys.

'Mummy when can we fill it?' Christopher asked impatiently as he bounced up and down with excitement.

'Soon darling, soon' she replied, as she spread it out, tugging the wooden seats into place. It looked as though there was a connecting piece missing on one of the corners.

Samantha stood up and searched in the bottom of the large cardboard box. The piece was not there. She scoured the lawn where she had unpacked it. It was quite a long piece so not likely to have disappeared into the grass.

'I'm just going into the garage Christopher to look for a piece that's missing, you stay here and get your toys ready for their swim, I won't be a minute.'

Samantha stepped over a flower bed onto the driveway and walked up to the garage where she took down the step ladder and propped it against the shelving so that she could climb up and begin the search. She stretched her hand over and could feel something down at the back of the shelf, she hitched herself up a bit higher and could see that the missing piece was lodged between the shelf and the garage wall. As she stretched to reach it the step ladder toppled, and she grabbed awkwardly at the framework, there was a moment of silence and then a groan as the shelving tilted away from the wall and began to fall. The boxes spilled out onto the garage floor and the metal shelving twisted and contorted itself as it followed.

As the dust settled, Samantha lay pinned down beneath a heavy piece of mdf. There was a metal upright digging into the back of her leg and her foot was pinned down by something out of sight. After a few moments she was able to move slightly and take stock of her injuries. She wriggled her fingers and toes and moved her head from side to side. Everything seemed okay with no pain as such, just a bump on the back of her head and an area of grazing on her right arm but she was unable to lift the heavy shelving, which meant she couldn't move from her position.

Outside at the bottom of the drive she could hear a vehicle pulling in, it sounded like a delivery van.

'Daddy, daddy,' she heard Christopher calling.

'No Christopher' she called out 'it can't be Daddy; he won't be home until bedtime.' Her voice was lost beneath the pile of wood and metal.

She strained to hear. She called out again, but then heard a noise, something between a shout and a squeal. She struggled to move but was trapped.

She heard the vehicle reversing out on to the lane before driving off.

Samantha struggled in terror to free herself, 'Christopher?' she screamed, 'Christopher!'

There was no reply, just birdsong coming from the trees along the driveway.

'Oh God, help me please' she cried out loud.

She pushed against the heavy shelf pinning her down and that was when she noticed the dark stain spreading out from underneath where she lay.

When Two Worlds Collide
by Dave Beer

This was written as a Writers' Group exercise, in which the story title is the title of a song, drawn at random from a list.

'OK your shot. Are you going to try to pot the green?'

'No. I reckon I'll go for blue,' Astraios scanned the table, working out angles and deflections just as his mentor, Helios, had taught him. 'If I miss the blue, the red is nicely in line, so it won't be a wasted shot.'

'Most of your shots are. Practically all of my score is courtesy of your mistakes,' commented Diemos, raising a snigger from the others.

'Why don't you aim for the yellow striped one? It's so much bigger, even you couldn't miss!' called Phobos, to a chorus of general laughter.

'Because it'll hardly move, even with this new super-heavy cue ball,' Astraios tried to maintain a dignified tone, amid hoots and cackles from the watchers in the room.

It wasn't so much a room as an auditorium, its walls so perfectly white that it was impossible to see the angles and corners, or even where they met the ceiling. Bright all-round lighting obliterated any shadows which might have considered lurking, giving the occupants a wraith-like lack of substance.

The centre of the room was dominated by what the players

referred to as 'The Table.' Not a very imaginative name for the basis of one of their favourite entertainments, but no worse than 'The Pitch,' or 'Play Station.' In fact, it wasn't a table at all, being a three-dimensional projection, lit from within by a huge yellow orb. Coloured balls of various sizes circled around the Table, and a myriad of oddly shaped bits and pieces got in the way, in a manner not totally random, so that many players believed they were controlled by some higher being. Others just put it down to Sod's Law.

Cue balls, again of various sizes, hovered obligingly around the periphery of The Table, and were selected by players according to the dynamics of play, tangential angular displacement probability, and most important, how pristinely white they were.

'Remember that pathetic little ball you chose a while ago, Aura?' Phaetheon, always game for a wind-up, couldn't help reminding everyone of that embarrassing shot in the previous game, when Aura had taken a beautifully accurate pot at the big yellow stripey one, which didn't even flinch. 'Your silly little cue ball disintegrated with a few little sparks and might never have existed.'

'Well at least it hit the target,' Aura rose to the bait. 'What about your effort in the previous series, eh? A huge cue ball you chose, and it still missed! You hardly managed to get it on The Table, it was so heavy. Ambled slowly across play, completely missed the stripey ball, glanced off the blue, knocking a huge chunk off it, and wiped out a species.'

'Good point, and well made' joined in Stilbon, always happy to have a go at Phaetheon. 'The Boss was furious. I thought HE was going to give you a damn good smiting. *Promising Species,* HE said, *Been the most successful for aeons,* HE said, *and I'd grown quite fond of their little scaly backs and long tails.'*

'HE did threaten to ban The Table if it happened again,' Aura reminded the assembled company, looking pointedly at Astraios as he lined up for his shot. She liked to unnerve the players, especially in tournament matches.

'A bit of left spin should do the trick, if you lot will shut up and let me concentrate,' Astraios tried to return to the game.

'What, so it'll spin off The Table, never to be seen again?' Phobos jeered, putting Astraios off his aim at the crucial moment. 'Ha ha, another point for Diemos.'

Phobos and Diemos had been companions since – well, forever, really. They took delight in vocal support for each other, usually in the form of barracking any opposition. And so, Astraios' mis-cued ball careered neatly between the blue and the red, silent but for the roar of laughter from the assembled company.

Diemos floated across to the scoreboard, triumphantly preparing to add another point to his total.

'Wait a minute, not so fast!' a commanding voice called across the room. 'That was a damn good shot, just watch as it plays out'

'Helios! I thought you were away. How nice to see you!' Astraios' relief at having an encouraging remark cast his way could not be disguised.

'Well, you know how it is, all sorts of things to attend to, people to bless, storms to invoke, around the place. But I wanted to make sure you go through to the finals, young Astraios. You have star qualities.' Helios moved to the bar, and poured himself a glass of Ambrosia, with ice. 'Never any bloody tonic here. I'll have to drink it neat, I suppose' he muttered, to no-one in particular.

Meanwhile, the errant cue-ball was heading directly towards the central orb of radiant light, accelerating as it slid through the smooth black velvet of The Table.

'That's definitely my point' Diemos chortled. 'Straight into the centre, ***Ping***, all gone, bring on the next cue ball.'

'Don't forget the spin,' Stilbon said, enigmatically. He usually aligned himself with Helios, and consequently with Astraios.

Except when Helios wasn't around.

The spin took the white ball around the central orb, instead of head on into it, gathering momentum as it hurtled back across The Table. The gap between the red and the blue had narrowed perceptibly, but the ball missed both as it streaked its way towards The Table's outer edge and disappeared.

'Exactly as I said it would' Phobos was ecstatic. He didn't often get things right, particularly when he himself was playing. Always a good feeling to predict someone else's doom.

'Don't be so sure,' said Astraios coolly. 'There is still plenty of time to observe the effects.'

Sure enough, the small distance between the red and the blue continued to decrease, infinitesimally slowly, but nevertheless perceptible to all in the room.

'They are indeed on a collision course.' Aura was predicting the point when the red and the blue would meet as they spiralled towards each other.

'I've got to hand it to you, that was a clever shot,' Diemos conceded with ill-disguised awe.

'That's my boy,' smirked Helios.

'You don't always have to score a direct hit to create the cataclysmic effect,' Astraios explained sagely, secretly amazed at his stroke of luck, and wondering if Helios had intervened in some way.

'Like the last game, eh?' Aura was good at reminding everyone of earlier *faux pas*. That fluffy cue ball that skimmed past the blue? That didn't hit anything, but the effects! Damned thing just melted, all over the blue, and didn't it rain? So much water; oceans of the stuff!'

'Rained for forty days and forty nights, I seem to recall' Helios chuckled.

'How do you know about such microscopic timescales?' Phaetheon had no real grasp of time as a measurable entity. Especially at the bar.

‘Oh, we all should know everything, as we are all Gods, aren’t we?’ Helios’ grandiose challenge ignored the fact that some of them had very specific areas of responsibility.

‘HE didn’t object to virtually wiping out lots of species that time, did HE?’

‘Why, Hello, Mephistopheles! Restored to your former glory, I see. But still the voice of dissent’ Aura recognised the grumbling tones of one of the Seniors.

‘If it wasn’t for that little guy with the big boat, the whole lot would have gone, and HE instructed it, as I recall!’

‘True, but HE was pretty pissed off with the lot of them. And who foiled HIS plans by giving the guy the tip-off?’ Aura raised an enquiring wing.

‘Enough of this banter!’ Sparks flew from Mephistopheles’ eyes, as they often did when he went off on one. ‘HIS revenge will work this time – they’ve really got on his tits with their H-Bombs, and I-pads and N-Power.’

‘N-Power?’

‘Yes, N-Power, and Global warming and wind turbines! Well, when this lot’s done, they’ll have wind turbines coming out of their ears – literally’ And a hot wind indicated that Mephistopheles was laughing – which unnerved everyone except Helios.

As the red and the blue continued their stealthy advance on each other towards their inevitable fate, Mephistopheles and Helios floated out of the room. Helios took a sip of Ambrosia, and lit up one of his favourite Stardust cigars. The two of them watched the smoke as it curled into a tight spiral, glittering with a hundred thousand million points of radiant light in the dense emptiness.

‘A majestic sight,’ commented Mephistopheles, cooling down a little.

‘It’s the deal,’ Helios replied.

‘Deal? What deal?’

'We create a whole new galaxy of potential life-cycles for every civilisation we destroy.'

Astraios	God of stars and planets
Phobos	Attendant to Mars
Diemos	Attendant to Mars
Helios	God of the Sun
Phaetheon	God of planet Jupiter
Aura	Goddess of the breeze
Stilbon	God of planet Mercury
Mephistopheles	The Devil

Frantic Owl

by Caroline Bennett

In one of those writing challenges where you unknowingly choose one another's punishment, I had to write a piece that included the phrases 'frantic owl' and 'complicated rug'.

'Mum! There's a frantic owl in my bedroom!'

Steph groaned and rolled over into her pillow.

'MUM!'

Kieran was prodding her with his teddy. Steph didn't lift her head but turned it towards him and opened one eye.

'Muuum! You got to come and see!'

'An owl? Really?'

Two eyes open. He put teddy against his heart and looked at her.

'Okay, okay. I'll come look.'

She pulled on a toweling dressing gown and trudged after him. At the door he stopped.

'You go first,' he said.

She pushed open the door. Immediately a large brown owl flapped its wings, flew across the room and crashed into the wardrobe. Steph shut the door.

'Holy crap!' She held the door shut with both hands as she turned to him. 'There is an owl!'

'And it's frantic!' Kieran replied.

'Damn right!'

'Muum. You're not supposed to swear in front of young children like me, in case I pick it up.'

'You won't. You're too sensible. And damn is only a little swear.'

'You said crap too.'

'I did. I'm sorry. The owl lowered my standards.'

'What are we going to do with the owl?' Kieran asked.

Steph pondered this question for a moment. She released one hand from the door handle.

'Can we keep it?'

'No.' Two hands back on the handle.

'Awww. Why not?'

'It's wild, it wouldn't want to live with us.'

Kieran looked at his bare feet and pulled his teddy to his throat.

'He might like it. Once he got used to it.'

'No hun, he's not a pet.'

Kieran chewed his lip.

Steph sighed. 'We don't even know if it is a he. It could be a girl owl.'

Kieran looked startled by this piece of information.

'Why would a girl owl come in my room?'

'I don't know...she was probably looking for food.'

'I don't think that's very likely. Owls eat mice and there are no mice in my room.'

'Well, then she got lost.'

'He didn't get lost. Owls can see in the dark very well.'

A loud crashing noise reminded them of the problem in the other room.

'Shall I ring Daddy?' Kieran asked.

'No.'

'He might come this time. If it's an owl emergency.'

'No hun.'

'But...'

'No.' Steph pulled the door to until it clicked. She looked at Kieran. 'Follow me.'

Ten minutes later they were back outside the bedroom door. Kieran was wearing a plastic bucket over his head with two eyes cut out. He had his winter coat on and two oven gloves over his hands. Teddy sat at a safe distance on the landing. Steph wore a cycling helmet and sunglasses.

Holding up a gardening-gloved finger Steph said to Kieran in a whisper, 'Okay, the plan is, we open the door slowly and both creep into the room. You keep the door shut. We do not want the owl getting onto the landing. I crawl on the floor, push the window open further, as far as it will go, then crawl back to you. We both try to scare the owl towards the window. Understand?'

The bucket nodded.

They opened the door a crack, squeezed through the narrow gap and shut it behind them. Steph peered into the moonlit room through her sunglasses. The owl sat on the windowsill, looking out at the garden. It turned towards them, turned back, and jumped into the night. Kieran and Steph ran forward to see the owl gliding silently away from the house.

'Can I sleep in your room tonight?'

'Okay hun.'

As they took off the owl protective equipment Kieran said, 'I don't think she got lost. I think she thought there were mice in my rug. It is all furry and dotty.'

'I thought you said owls could see in the dark very well.'

'They can. But it is a very complicated rug.'

March 2020

by Joanne Stubbs

Inspired by the events of March 2020

At the reception desk in the garage, the only hint that anything has changed is a dispenser bottle filled with viscous pink liquid that sits on the counter. Someone has scribbled 'visitors' along its length in marker pen.

The man behind the counter has a round nose. He smiles and takes the car keys off me without a flinch, saying he'll call when the service is complete. I wonder whether I should have come, but then I think of the people without work if everyone cancelled.

While I'm out I hope no one coughs or sneezes, myself included, but coming back into bright sunlight makes my nose itch. It's the start of hay fever season and the trees are bursting with golden catkins. Does that explain my runny nose?

Further down the road, where it steepens towards town, an older couple don't smile. They step off the pavement to avoid me, frowning over the collars of their waterproofs. I want to tell them I'm not a threat, but I could be.

I feel good walking in the sun, and a little subversive. The roads are quiet. Birds chirp, primroses speckle the churchyard, and a fat wood pigeon bends the wires between telegraph poles. She preens, one wing out for balance, and I hope she doesn't poo on me as I walk beneath. She knows nothing of this human situation, except that the air might be clearing now that flights are grounded and so many commutes have ceased. Home offices are irrelevant to pigeons.

In My Hand a Hag Stone
by Joan Bartholomew

Inspired by finding these strange stones while walking on the beaches in Norfolk.

In my hand a hag stone.
Grey, a skull, a whale, the hole, sea made, eye socket
Brown gash, mouth, dappling, hair.
Smelling still of the North Sea, tasting of salt.

In my hand a hag stone.
Held left-handed, I move my thumb deosil, the witches' way it might grant a wish.
Hang it on an iron nail over the stable door
It will keep the witches from the horses.

In my hand a hag stone.
Thread a most precious thing on it I will never lose it,
Hang it on the heavy, plough horse's head, it will keep him from harm,
If I want the singing fisher boy to have a good catch and come back safely,
I necklace it round the bow of his boat.

In my hand a hag stone.
Look through it there are fairies.
Under my bed it will stop the pain that comes from the Hag despair, sitting heavy on my heart.
If I give it with love, you are safe and lost no more, and will come back to me.
In my hand a hag stone.

Too Many Doors
by Alan Shrimpton

Another exercise was to create a piece of short fiction that incorporated a well-known quote from the movies. I think the rest of the Group expected me to use something from a science fiction movie (my favourite genre) but I decided to do something completely different. The quote comes right at the end so you may guess it before you get there.

'What do you mean there's no pub for lunch on this bloody walk?'

'I told you there wasn't yesterday,' I said, stopping to look back. My mate Tony Thompson, 'Toto' to his friends, was lagging slightly to emphasise how disgruntled he was. 'There's a perfectly good pub, I continued, 'just before we get back to the car so we can have a pint to celebrate finishing the walk.'

'Can't believe you picked a walk with no pub,' he grumbled.

'Sorry,' I said and resumed walking. I wasn't sorry because drinking with Tony at lunchtimes had caused quite a few plans to be modified, and even some events to be missed entirely. The man could drink which, despite my best intentions, meant so did I when I was in his company. Better to avoid the possibility, sometimes at least.

'Think how much you'll enjoy that first pint when we've finished the walk,' I said.

'That's bloody miles away,' said Tony. 'What's wrong with

having a beer at the half-way point?' He asked.

'Because it's never just 'a' beer,' I called back. 'Sometimes, we just need to enjoy the walk, look at the scenery and…'. I trailed off as I turned a corner and saw a long stone building with a high timbered roof just off the trail ahead. There was a painted sign hanging over the doorway which said 'The Many Doors'.

I stopped and stared because there was nothing marked in the map and yet this looked pretty much like…'

'A pub,' yelled Tony as he caught up to me. 'I should have known you were having me on you bastard. Come on,' he called striding past me with more energy than he had shown so far today and a big grin on his face. 'First round's on you for trying to make me think there wasn't a pub.' He pushed through the door.

'There aren't any damn pubs on this walk,' I called, but hurried after him. 'I've no idea what this place is, it's probably…

'A pub,' said Tony with obvious delight.

And it clearly was. There was a huge circular bar in the middle of the room with lots of nooks and alcoves around the wall, some of them occupied. But it was dark as well. That sort of ageing, low beamed, steeped in history kind of darkness where all you could really see was the bar.

'Man could die of thirst while you stand there,' said Tony. 'Get your wallet out.'

Tony walked to the bar. The barman was a little short but powerfully built and I got the impression that you wouldn't want to argue with him at closing time. He was friendly enough though.

'Two pints of your very best ale,' said Tony. He nodded his head in my direction. 'He's paying.'

Two pints were drawn from a cask behind the bar and deposited in front of us. One was immediately sampled by Tony. Well, half emptied actually.

'Bloody hell,' he exclaimed. 'That's gorgeous.'

And it was. Really good. First pints were quickly finished, and second ones ordered. We leant on the bar and took in our surroundings.

'So, why'd you tell me there were no pubs?' said Tony smacking his lips in appreciation of his second ale which had almost disappeared.

'Because there weren't,' I said, 'or weren't supposed to be anyways. This is all a bit odd.'

'Dickhead,' said Tony, amiably, and returned to his beer.

I continued to look around the bar room. It was big and gloomy, though not without atmosphere. But mostly big. In fact, it was a damn sight bigger than it looked from outside. I stared at my beer and wondered how strong it was. And then I noticed the doors. There were a lot of them, scattered between the alcoves, but just as I started to point them out to Tony, one of them opened.

A man walked into the bar. Nothing odd in that except he was wearing leathers. I don't mean motorcycle leathers, which would have been odd enough halfway up a Lakeland fell, but laced jerkin and trews with knee high boots, and he was wearing a bloody big sword on his back. He had… presence.

'Toto,' I whispered, 'have you seen…'

'Yep,' he said. 'Cool outfit. Is there a movie set around here?' He stared.

'There's not supposed to be anything around here,' I said, 'just the trail.'

Yeah, well you got that wrong, didn't you,' smirked Tony. 'He's either filming something or he's a re-enactor of some kind. You know, like the Sealed Knot or something. Either way, he bloody nailed the outfit.'

The barman hurried over to the newcomer.

'That's your considered opinion,' I said. 'Really?'

'No,' said Tony, quietly. He put his pint down, something unheard of in any normal lunchtime drinking session.

'And now I come to look,' he continued quietly, 'have you seen the guy in the cloak over there?' He nodded towards a hooded figure in one of the alcoves, who suddenly looked in our direction.

'Toto,' I whispered, 'do you think perhaps we should be making a move?'

'Yep,' he said, downing the remains of his pint, 'I think this place is a little weird.' I don't think Tony had ever described a single pub as 'weird' previously, but I knew what he meant.

'Another one,' said the barmaid, who had appeared noiselessly at our end of the bar. And she was a proper barmaid too. Curly auburn hair, pretty, low cut blouse, the works. Just my type in fact, if you ignored the pointy ears.

'Ah, no,' I stammered. 'Thank you. Got a long way to go yet.' I pulled Tony away from the bar.

She smiled.

'Another time then,' she said. 'Can you find your door again?'

'I think we can find the door,' I said. 'Thank you.' I steered Tony away from temptation and pushed him through the door.

'That was also weird,' he said. 'I mean, why did she say, 'your door'? We've not had that much to drink.' He shook his head. 'Have we?'

And perhaps we had because I suddenly noticed that the track we were now standing on was much better made than the Lakeland trail we had been following before we got to the pub. And there were trees on either side of the path where we'd been on open fell beforehand. And that's to say nothing of the archer, dressed in green and silver, who nodded amiably at us as he strode past us and into the Inn. He had pointy ears too I noticed.

'What the… where the hell are we?' asked Tony. He stopped and stared around.

'I don't know Toto, but we're a long way from Kansas,' I said.

Pike

by Tim Melling

This was a story that I wrote as an antidote to the James Herriot stories. It began as an exercise on a writing course that I attended but then I continued to work on it at home and at Writers Group.

The curtains opened with a sigh, beechwood hoop on beechwood pole. Outside the window, single glazed, corroded metal frame, cream paint peeling, a soft drizzle was falling. Ink black crows cawed and croaked, wary of a circling buzzard. It was cold and even though the fire was on, a wintry chill penetrated my sweater. In my hand a letter, telling of the death of a friend; and a distant voice calling me from years past.

I was younger then, just eleven, and my best friend was Daniel, the butcher's son.

'Dad and me are going to Thirsk market' he said. 'We're going to buy some beef cattle'. I waited, knowing what was coming.

'I'll help Dad slaughter them. We have our own,' he hesitated, searching for the word, 'abattoir. Want to come?' Even then he spoke at a lower register than was natural for his age. 'He's a little old man;' said his aunt, 'very proper is our Daniel.'

'No thanks Pike, I'm off fishing with Jack.' Daniel earned the nickname on a fishing expedition after he landed a pike that bit him on the arm; 'Look, you can see the meat,' showing off his wound.

Daniel's Dad was Joe. Jet black hair swept back off his forehead; glossed in place with Brilliantine. Every now and then, a rogue crow's wing would fall over one eye, lending him a piratical air. He was a gentle, softly spoken man with a direct and clear look. It said 'I tell the truth and I know the truth when I hear it.' He was respected.

One long day, at a loose end, I was dawdling down the road, bored, no one about and nowt doing. The Spring sunshine was warm, and daffodils were waving seas of yellow in the proudly neat gardens; the scent of Spring was everywhere. Daniel's cat, Smokey, appeared from the border under their living room window; I had a moment of madness.

The stone felt smooth and nicely weighted in my hand; the cat ten yards away. I took aim and threw the stone, as hard as I could. Missed the cat, hit the window which shattered, deliberately I felt, in a relentless crystal avalanche.

Joe appeared around the side of the house. He stopped, surveyed the damage, and saw me by the wall. He was calm. 'What happened young man?'

'I.......I,' I faltered. Unable to confess the truth, I burst into tears and said 'There was a squirrel by the garage door and I threw a stone at it and missed.'

A bad lie and he knew it. He let it go, though, and said he wouldn't tell my Mum and Dad, but he thought I should. I did, as soon as I dared. I don't know how it was settled. He was that sort of man. Never angry, but clear and firm. Daniel loved his Dad.

Joe died suddenly that summer. I learned later he had what people called 'a weak heart'. It shocked everyone. He was a big hearted man.

I didn't see Daniel until the day of the funeral. He walked stiffly to a shiny black limo behind the hearse. His blond hair brushed neatly to one side, wearing long trousers, a tweed jacket, a white shirt, and black tie, he helped his grieving mum and sister, Jenny, to the car. I learned later that he had not cried once. On hearing the news of his father's death, he had turned to his mum and said, 'Don't worry Mum, I'll take care of us all now.' He was eleven.

The day was warm and pleasant, and a soft breeze played among the flowers. It was good that the sun shone; funerals in the rain are harder to take. I remembered the wet, cold funeral of my grandfather with the wind blowing shredded clouds of rain across the bleak hillside cemetery.

After the funeral I didn't see Daniel for several weeks. The summer passed in a warm haze and hot August turned into warm September. Then the rains came in October.

One wet Saturday afternoon, he just turned up and asked if I wanted to go round to see his new tape recorder. 'It's got a microphone so we can record a song'.

I don't remember much about that afternoon, not the tape recorder nor the song; I do remember how different Pike was.

'Mother, fetch tea please,' to his mother. 'Jenny, get out; we will be busy for the next hour,' to his younger sister. Jenny got out and his mother fetched tea.

'Right Tom, shall we get on then?'

'Right, Pike' I replied.

'Don't call me Pike, Tom. It's Daniel, not Pike, Daniel. Your turn with the microphone…. Come on, get on with it.'

Other people noticed a change in Daniel too; wilder, reckless, unmoored. Bill Jaiks was an alcoholic English teacher who would wobble up the road on an old bike with his battered leather satchel, a beret on his head and wearing a patched tweed jacket.

'Pissed again, Mr Jaiks?' Daniel taunted him.

'Me too son' sighed Bill Jaiks. Daniel scowled; he resented being outsmarted.

Mrs Jaiks called on Daniel's mother to complain about his

'rude and disrespectful behaviour'. Daniel opened the door and rudely and disrespectfully sent her on her way.

I envied Daniel his freedom. Untroubled by deadlines, or parental standards of behaviour, he made his own rules and became a popular if unpredictable figure.

We lost touch for a few years; I heard he had qualified as a vet and was working in a practice in North Yorkshire. Then I had a phone call from his mother.

'He often mentions you' she said. 'Your mother keeps me up to date with what you are doing'. Then, out of the blue, 'Will you go and see him, talk to him? Find out what happened. He won't tell me anything.'

A month before, Daniel had married a girl his mother didn't know. No one was invited. Daniel's Mum didn't even know her name.

He lived in a flat above the surgery. When I arrived, there was no sign of anyone else. The living room had a shabby unkempt air; a couple of old easy chairs with worn threadbare arms and greasy back rests that smelled of old hair lacquer. 'I thought you were married?'

'I was' he said and stopped. Anger flashed across his face. He looked at me, 'She's gone.' Nothing more. I started to ask a question. He raised his hand; 'I've got to go and put down a dog. Do you want to come?'

We drove to a dog rescue home near Pateley Bridge. It was a clean well run place and the owner was a cheerful, rosy faced woman who loved her animals. 'We've re-homed this dog twice' she said, pointing to a lively young golden Labrador. 'But he is just so destructive'. The dog was looking at us, tail wagging and yelping.

'He destroyed the kitchen in his most recent house. The owners brought him back; couldn't do a thing with him. And they have always had dogs.'

'OK bring him over then' said Daniel, and looked at me,

anger flashing again in his eyes.

The dog approached him. 'Hello boy,' he said and ruffled his neck. The dog tried to lick Daniel. 'There's a good boy. Tom, can you hold his paw for me?'

I took the dog's paw. Daniel rummaged in his scuffed brown leather bag, brought out a razor, a small bottle and a syringe. He carefully shaved a section of the dog's leg. He opened the bottle, plunged the needle in and drew out the clear liquid into the syringe. He pushed the needle into a vein in the dog's leg and pressed the plunger until the syringe was empty. The dog slumped over and was gone.

'What I can't stand' said Daniel on the way back, 'is an owner who doesn't train a dog properly. Labradors are not difficult to train. The first owner just let him run wild, no discipline, no socialisation training. Nothing. They just let him do whatever he wanted and now the poor bloody dog has paid the price. It should be the owner who is put down, not the bloody dog!' He was shouting now. I looked across at him. He was staring ahead, his mouth curled in a silent snarl, angry tears running down his face. 'Sometimes life is just not bloody fair.'

He never mentioned his first marriage again. I don't even know if it was true.

Two years later Daniel married Angie. It was a happier time. Angie was smart, quick, with a mischievous sense of humour. She needed that with Daniel. It wasn't easy.

The next few years passed in a blur for all of us. Children arrived, careers got serious, parents got old, ill, and then died.

The last time I saw Daniel, he helped me scatter my parents' ashes at Brigg Flats in the Howgills. Daniel, Angie and their two children had moved to the area some years before and bought a large animal practice at the foot of the fells. They lived in an old stone farmhouse, heavy Cumbrian stone, slate roofs and mossy walls on the lee side. He'd converted two barns into a veterinary surgery and operating theatre; he seemed settled.

The kids were happy in school and Angie looked after the books.

Briggs Flat was my parents' favourite place for its sense of peace, solace, and healing. It was a comfort to have him with me; gruff, curmudgeonly, Dan knew how I was feeling; we drank a pint of bitter together afterwards. Not much was said, at first. The pints loosened us and warmed the chat. 'I thought you had a thriving equine practice in the Cotswolds?' I asked. He played a straight bat. 'I did, but it didn't work out in the end. How are things with you?'

I learned later that Daniel's colleagues in the Equine practice had rebelled against his 'controlling' manner and resigned en masse. He'd had a nervous breakdown; legal action was taken and he lost both the practice and a lot of money.

When we said goodbye, I watched him walk back to his car. He carried himself in exactly the same way as he'd done on the day of his father's funeral. Ramrod straight back and a careful way of walking as if the ground beneath him couldn't be trusted to hold him and might give way at any moment. I thought 'How bruised and battered you are. Still 'limping into the blizzard.' It is as if you are anticipating the worst and then it crushes you. You have never asked for help and you don't see that your friends love you.'

Two years later I learned from Angie that she and the children had left home as he had 'become impossible, rigid and unbending; prone to eruptions of anger at the smallest things.'

Daniel cut a lonely figure in the area. He kept a few sheep and spent his spare time taking care of his flock on the blustery moors. Her final letter arrived today and told me that, one blizzarding December night, he walked out of his front door, across the yard, through the old wooden gate into the lane and up onto the fell. He didn't return. He was found some days later, sitting with his back to an old bare oak, his sightless eyes open, looking over towards his sheep, safe in their pen.

The last time I visited Brigg Flats, the oak tree that marked the place where we had scattered my parents' ashes had vanished, washed away in the January floods. Daniel had wanted to be an oak for his mother and sister. If only he could have been a willow.

You Sat Close to Me with Your Hand on my Arm
by Anna Quartly

You sat close to me with your hand on my arm,
breathing deeply with a sloping head;
resting assured and protecting me from harm.

As the sun withers and the wind reads a psalm,
we share a moment of sleep on your bed;
you sat close to me with your hand on my arm.

I remember the good, old days on our farm,
chomping through the crusts of bread;
resting assured and protecting me from harm.

The cheeks I smell are sprayed with charm,
the silence that weaves between us like thread;
you sat close to me with your hand on my arm.

And now we wait for the sound of the alarm,
opening our eyes and looking ahead;
resting assured and protecting me from harm.

To find your hand close to my palm,
vanishing the dread that was unshed;
you sat close to me with your hand on my arm,
resting assured and protecting me from harm.

Mother Dear
by Anne Sheppard

This piece was inspired by an evening where we all brought something that we were working on to the group meeting. The idea being for it to be critiqued by the other group members and re-written after taking on board what had been said. This is the final (and third) version of that original piece

---

It had been an unsettling sort of day so far, and the visit to the coroner's office to pick up her mother's death certificate had taken longer than she had thought it would. Shirley ran now, puffing up the stairs to the 3rd floor of the hospital, the arrows guiding her towards the reception desk where she handed in her appointment letter before heading down the corridor to find the waiting area with its rows of blue plastic-coated chairs.

'Why do they have such awful furniture in these places?' she muttered to herself as she sat down.

After collecting the death certificate Shirley had sat in her car for several minutes, breathing deeply to calm herself. She had been nervous at the inquest and still felt uncomfortable every time she thought of it; by the time her breathing had returned to normal, and she focused again upon her surroundings, she realised that she would need to drive quickly if she was going to get to her appointment on time.

Her mother Joyce had been a difficult woman but after she

lost her sight 3 years earlier, she had become downright impossible. Shirley being an only child had felt obliged to give up her secretarial job and stay at home to care for her ageing mother, and for the first couple of years all had been well, but gradually the whining and the carping had become unbearable. The constant effort of caring for her mother, the lack of any life of her own and the sleepless nights had started to affect her own health, and she had been suffering recently from headaches and bouts of double vision; Shirley had convinced herself that she had diabetes – she would get confirmation today as she was seeing the consultant to go through the results of the tests that had been carried out.

After hearing Shirley's description of the events prior to her mother's tragic death the coroner had returned a verdict of accidental death. Shirley had told him that she hadn't meant to push her mother down the stairs; she had pushed her away because Joyce had lashed out as she often did and Shirley had put up her hands in defence, forgetting that they were on the top landing by the enclosed narrow staircase.

Joyce had gone down backwards, and as she had fallen she had flung out her arms, catching hold of the handrail with one hand; this had stopped her from falling all the way down but as Shirley had explained, her mother's weight and bulk had meant that she had been unable to pull herself up or turn herself around, and there was no way to get behind her to help support her or help lower her to the ground floor.

Shirley told the coroner that she had tried to persuade Joyce to take her hand so that she could hold on to her and help lower her slowly down the stairs, but that her mother had shrieked every time she felt her daughter coming near. For some time, they had remained there, at an impasse.

The coroner had accepted her story completely and with a great deal of sympathy. He understood that eventually Joyce had had to let go of the handrail and that because she had done it without any warning Shirley had been unable to immediately grab her hand and so she had catapulted down the stairs breaking her neck in the process.

The only negative comment he had made was to ask Shirley why she hadn't tried to attract the attention through the attic window, of a neighbour or someone passing by who could perhaps have broken into the house and approached Joyce from the bottom of the stairs. Shirley had replied tearfully that she had thought of that afterwards and would never forgive herself for not having done so.

Everyone had been marvellously kind and now that she had the death certificate the funeral could take place, and she would be able to get on with her life at long last after all those years of caring for the cantankerous old bitch! She stretched out her legs and admired the red high heels that she had bought that morning. She had already booked a cruise and was meeting the builder later that afternoon to arrange for some much-needed improvements to the house.

She laughed inwardly at how gullible everyone had been; it had been so easy to push her mother down the stairs! Yes, Joyce had grabbed the handrail as she had told them, but she had failed to mention that she had also willingly taken her daughter's hand only to have it quickly dropped so that Shirley could pick up her legs and flip her backwards down the staircase. Shirley hugged the memory to herself; she would never forget the sound of her mother's neck breaking – the sound of freedom!

'Miss Paget?'

Shirley looked up at the young nurse standing in the doorway, she nodded and getting to her feet followed her along the corridor to a door where she was invited to enter.

'Ah Miss Paget, please come in,' said Mr. Gale, half rising from his seat as he indicated a chair in front of him.

Shirley seated herself, ready to hear the results of the tests and the dietary recommendations to follow.

Mr. Gale placed his hands in the prayer position and leaned towards her slightly. 'Miss Paget, we have a problem.'

Shirley sat back in her seat and looked blankly at Mr. Gale, but he was staring down at his notes.

'A problem?' she asked, her voice strained as her mouth became suddenly dry. The scent of eau de cologne swept over her, and Shirley gave an involuntary shiver, it was the scent her mother had always used.

Mr. Gale turned the pages of the file on the desk.

'Yes, the tests have all come back confirming my initial suspicion regarding the diagnosis.' He paused and looked at her over the top of his glasses.

'Yes,' she said, 'so what is it you are saying?'

'I'm very sorry to say that you have a hereditary ocular disease that stems from a genetic late onset malfunction of the optic nerve – the same thing that your mother suffers from.'

Shirley sat in stunned silence. Mr. Gale continued to look at her. He coughed slightly and Shirley's concentration returned to the room and to what she had just been told.

'My mother died' said Shirley stiffly, 'I've just been to pick up the death certificate.'

'I'm so sorry, I didn't know,' said the consultant, reddening slightly.

'So, I'm going to lose my sight then,' said Shirley defiantly. 'How long do you think before that happens? I mean my mother was in her 80's before it happened to her and I'm not 50 yet.'

Mr. Gale pursed his lips and shook his head. 'No, no, you have nothing to worry about, catching it early means it is treatable. You will need to have a course of injections followed by eye drops and tablets and we will have you back in three months for a check-up. You will receive all the information and the dates for the appointments in the post.'

Shirley let out a big sigh and stood up. 'Thank you so much' she said as she picked up her handbag and walked towards the door.

Outside in the corridor Shirley allowed herself a moment to compose herself. The consultant had given her a fright; losing her sight would be unbearable. She walked on, through the swing doors at the end of the corridor and began walking down the stairs back to the car park. She failed to notice the piece of plastic film lying on the floor until her heel caught in it. She hopped on one leg reaching down to pull it free. Below a door slammed and there was movement in the air around her. The stairwell filled with the scent of eau de cologne as Shirley teetered on her heels and fell.

Weddings Nowadays
by Jane Gray-Wallis

I do love a wedding. It wasn't all that long ago that weddings were very different. The couple were often young, rarely had lived together. The wedding was usually followed by a lunch then the couple would leave in the middle of the afternoon. Gifts were all the basic things you needed to set up a house.

Weddings nowadays, call me old fashioned, but I don't go in for these newfangled weddings.

I mean, take Eleanor for instance, my niece Eleanor. She'd been going out with her Robbie, let me see ….. well, it must be eight years now. Moved in with him when she was six months gone. Then proudly announced, proudly mind, that they would think about getting married when the children were old enough to enjoy it.

In my day, the marriage came first. Nor was there any of this going on all day into the small hours. I suppose our wedding was a quiet one, even then. Just the church, then a lunch with our close relatives and parent's friends, then off on the train at half past three. Our first night together was at a little hotel in Bristol. It might have been a bit less shocking if we had known each other better. Perhaps if I had known what to expect but you didn't discuss those things in those days. All my mother said to me was that Freddie would know what to do.

‘We’re having a humanist wedding,’ Eleanor said. Well that sent my sister in to a flat spin because you don’t know what to expect do you. I mean, at least with a church wedding everyone knows their role. I always think it’s more satisfying with the Vicar leading the way. Eleanor said she’d had enough of him leading the way. Such rudeness, you don’t know where it comes from do you?

I must say it was a very jolly affair. Such a lot of young people, all gaily decked out, dancing the night away. She was right, the children did enjoy it.

I would have liked to have danced on my wedding night. It might have helped. But then I wasn’t to know that what Freddie liked, was a bit unusual. He had been in the Far East with the Navy, you know, I think they do things a bit differently there. It might have been easier if we’d had children but that wasn’t to be. The Doctor reckoned I’d caught something that stopped it happening. He didn’t say how I’d caught it.

Eleanor’s gone off to the Caribbean, truly the whole family kids and all. She showed me the pictures last Christmas when she came to visit; all laughing on the beach.

Freddie and I had our picture taken. It’s a bit scratched now but there we are on the front at Weston-super-Mare. I’m clinging to his arm and peering at the lens. He’s looking away – out to sea.

The Abbey Church
by Alison Jackson

Inspired by one of Alison's many visits to Iona.

They asked for volunteers and took the first who offered.
And so we gathered in the crossing,
arranged ourselves according to the rite
and processed through the chancel.

The priest.
Two with bread.
Two with wine.
One with the great brass platter for the offering.

We placed them on the altar, moved behind, beside it.
We performed the age-old ritual in this place
where, for fifteen hundred years,
Church of Scotland ministers, Benedictine monks,
Saint Columba,
have consecrated,
served the bread and wine,
received the people's gifts.
The rite accomplished, we returned
in procession down the chancel, carrying what remained.

The priest.
Two with bread.
Two with wine.
One with the gifts of the congregation.

In the cloisters afterwards
a woman from another land hugged me, weeping tears of joy,
for she had lived her dream, impossible at home,
when, by chance – or was it chance? –,
six women
consecrated bread and wine, and served them to the people
gathered
on Sunday morning
in the Abbey
on Iona.

Auntie's House

by Caroline Bennett

Written after being encouraged to try writing for children.

Molly stared up at the old house. Molly's mum rang the doorbell for a second time and looked at her watch. A scuffling, shifting noise of boxes moving came from behind the front door. 'I'm coming' called a muffled voice. More shuffling cardboard. Finally, the voice shouted 'Can you come to the other door? This one is a little hard to get to.'

Molly's mother sighed and waded through the waist high grass balancing a cake tin under her arm. Molly followed on; her rucksack heavy on her back. Several fat cats bounded alongside them in the meadow that was Auntie's garden.

The back door was wide open and in the kitchen, standing between piles of magazines and boxes of glass jars was Auntie May grinning and waving. Auntie never commented on how you'd grown or hugged you straight away. She glanced at Molly and turned to find the kettle among a mess of cookery books and piled crockery. Over tea and cake, Molly's shyness slipped away. Mum chatted about the plans for Harry's friend's camping trip and her own holiday in Spain with The New Boyfriend.

By the time Mum had driven away Molly was feeling quite excited about staying with Auntie. Auntie May showed the room she had cleared for her. A neat clean bed with a beautiful quilt and frilly edged pillowcase. A tall bookcase full of books. Auntie May pointed to them. 'I moved all the books I thought you might like into here. I moved everything else onto the landing, so the piles there might be a little precarious. Leave your bag in here – I expect you might like to explore the house?'

Auntie May didn't seem to have rules. She did give occasional warnings though. 'Oh – yes, sorry Molly – the ginger one does bite sometimes' 'That door is a bit stuck – give it a kick if it won't open' 'Be careful of your fingers –there's a broken vase in that drawer'. Molly began to understand why Mum hadn't let Harry come and stay with Auntie too.

In every room there were objects Molly had never seen before. 'Why do you have this?' Molly asked, holding up a stuffed dead crow. And then Auntie would tell a story. About the strange and wonderful world, full of things that nobody loved, and nobody understood. She let Molly play with an old typewriter, each key hitting a piece of paper hard through a ribbon of ink. A sewing machine that you wobbled your foot to work and the cloth in your hands raced away to the other side.

And books. Books like Molly had never seen. With stories, facts, poems, pictures, maps, photographs, and paintings. Molly read so much she couldn't remember what was real. One book was different from the others. It had a hard black cover with swirly patterns twisted over it. Inside was a language Molly didn't know. She took it to Auntie May. Auntie looked puzzled. 'I don't remember it – I must have picked it up somewhere?'

Molly couldn't stop looking at the book. She carried it about the house and looked inside the pages again and again. She lay under a tree in the garden, a warm cat on her lap, and traced her fingers over the unfamiliar shaped letters. That night, Molly kissed Auntie May goodnight and took the book to her room. She lay in bed and turned page after page, reading without understanding. Sometimes, she felt a feeling, as though the story was readable after all. The next page she turned revealed a secret. A crisp, flat plant pressed within the pages. Molly looked at it carefully and replaced it against the pages of the book. She looked over the symbols and an incredible sadness turned inside her. Maybe no one would ever understand these words. This story would go untold by whoever had written it. A tear rolled down her nose and fell onto the open page against the dry leaves of the pressed plant.

Molly dreamt that night of a sucking, tearing monster, moving through the house. In the morning she awoke and thought it was still night. It was dark and warm in her room. Trying to get out of bed, she realised something was stopping her. Dense hard stems filled the room. They had punched holes in the floor and roof. Leaves pressed against the window, absorbing light and shading the room inside.

Molly wriggled through a gap in the jungle and squeezed her way to Auntie's room. They crawled between thick branches down the stairs and climbed out of the living room window.

The house was covered in plant. People in the street stared and pointed at the house as they walked by. Leaves stretched from the twisting stems through the roof towards the sky.

Auntie May stared up at her house. 'Would you like me to call your father?' she asked. 'No thank you' said Molly firmly. 'I suppose we'll just have to chop it back a bit' said Auntie May. Armed with axes from the shed, Molly and Auntie May cut at the stems. They were woody inside and took some force to break apart. They worked hard all day, stopping only to scramble through vines in the kitchen to search for lunch and cat biscuits. By late afternoon they had cleared a path from the back door to the hallway. 'We'll tackle the living room tomorrow,' said Auntie.

They slept under the moon on a blanket in the long grass garden. The night was warm and Molly cuddled up to the cat that did not bite.

In the morning, they went to start work on the living room. But the path they had cleared had regrown. The plant had even more leaves and the stems had refilled the kitchen right up to the back door.

Just as they were trying to work out what to do next three men turned up in a large van. One had a suit and a clipboard. The other two wore blue overalls and hard black boots. The man with the clipboard turned to Auntie May, 'We've had complaints about your garden,' he said. 'We've come to clear it'.

The man made notes on his clipboard and directed the other two men to measure the leaves and stems. As they did, brown furry buds appeared on the plant all over the house. They stopped work for lunch 'Slow work this, I don't know how you could let it get so out of hand' said one to Auntie May. The men sat in their van eating sandwiches and drinking tea from a flask.

Auntie May and Molly lay in the long grass and looked up at the towering jungle. The brown buds began to split open and pink flowers emerged all over the house. A bird flew from a tree in the garden and landed on an open flower. It tilted its head and drank from the centre of the petals. More birds came and they moved from one flower to another. The four cats jumped in the air trying to catch them. They chattered their teeth, making strange noises as the flocks of birds flew safe above their heads.

The men in overalls came back and brought a chainsaw with them from the van. They pulled a cord, and a loud, jagged noise scared the birds away. The cats ran to Auntie and Molly who bent down to rub behind their ears. The men started cutting through the thick stems and the whining saw sliced through them quickly. But wherever they cut, more shoots started to appear. Leaves sprouted from new stems branching from places they had damaged. High above them pink flower petals were falling to the ground and twisting pink pods were opening, spilling hard black seeds onto the lawn. After they had worked for a few hours the man with the clipboard and measuring tape returned and called them over. They stood back from the house. 'It's no good. It's growing faster than you can cut it. We'll have to burn it.'

One of the men in overalls lit a single long match. His hand hovered through the front door letterbox and then he dropped the burning match into Auntie May's home. They heard crackling and smelled smoke. Standing on the other side of the street Auntie May and Molly watched the fire spread quickly through the house. Orange light glowed at the windows. The leaves of the plant shrivelled and turned to ash. Some glass exploded onto the road. Auntie pulled Molly further away.

After a few hours, the stone skeleton of the house was all that remained. Auntie May sat on the kerb with her feet in the gutter, her cats winding round her. She covered her face with her hands. 'My books, my poor books' she cried. Molly put her arm around Auntie but didn't know what to say. The man ticked something on his clipboard and the three men got into the large white van and drove away.

They had a bad night's sleep in the ash covered garden with the disgruntled cats prodding them in the back. Molly woke before Auntie May. The house was there, a hollow wreck – but in the garden there were new shoots of the plant coming up all over the lawn.

Molly shook Auntie awake. They ate a breakfast of biscuits from the corner shop and wandered around the outside of the house, looking at the young plants from every angle. The plants grew as they watched and soon were taller than Molly, and then Auntie May. As they walked their third circuit of the garden Molly noticed something strange growing from one of the plants. The typewriter, complete with paper was sprouting between the leaves. They looked and looked, and more and more objects started appearing on the plants around them. Stacks of newspaper hung under leaves, the stuffed crow perched on a stem and a broken ornament pushed through from an opening bud. The grandfather clock stood in the lawn, pulling down a branch and the fridge, full of food, seemed to be working without being connected to any electricity. Books were everywhere. Auntie hugged Molly and laughed 'It's all here!'

They went into the house. There were no signs of plant, but the cats were enjoying running around the blackened rooms. 'It needs a good clean' said Auntie May 'but it will be easier because it's empty'. They spent the rest of the day scrubbing walls and Auntie called some people from the phone growing in the garden. She made appointments for them to fix the windows, the roof and the floor.

They moved some camp beds into the empty house and Molly stared at the stars through a hole in the roof before she fell asleep.

The next day they did another tour of the garden. The plants did not seem to have grown any taller. Auntie May looked for a long time at a stack of newspaper. Finally, she picked it off the plant and carried it to the pavement. 'I think it's time I recycled those' she said 'I'll never catch up reading them now'.

Each day Auntie May put a few things back inside the house and threw one small pile of things away. Molly and Auntie were on their way back from taking some books to the charity shop when they spotted Mum's car parked outside the house. 'Oh dear' said Auntie 'It must be Thursday already'. Molly's mum stood in the garden, staring. Auntie May greeted her. 'Beautiful plants aren't they? I've decided I'm going to keep them.'

After an hour, Molly and her Mum drove away from the house. Auntie May stood in the garden full of her possessions and waved goodbye. Molly waved hard with both hands from the back window of the car. A breeze pushed through the garden and the leaves of the plants waved too.

Ieuan's Barrow

by Alan Jackson

This piece was inspired by a road in Peru that we drove to get to an important historical site. When I was younger, I knew someone like Ieuan whose instinctive generosity helped me through a difficult time. This story is a very tiny thank you to him and to all the Ieuans out there.

Ieuan was a big lad – especially his hands and his head – but as gentle as a falling leaf. Quite literally, he would not hurt a fly, except a fly that was bothering his Mam, of course; it was the only time he was ever angry, when someone upset his Mam, and then, well, nobody did it twice. Ieuan was a very big lad.

Schoolwork was never going to be his thing; that was obvious from the start. He could talk but reading and writing were well beyond him; he could just recognise his own name, Ieuan, and eventually he could even begin to scrawl it, but that was his limit. Anything he could do, though, especially anything to help someone, that he loved; and talking, he would talk to anyone, anyone at all who would listen – and usually people did; everybody liked Ieuan; it was almost impossible not to. Ieuan was a big lad, but he was so gentle, so happy to help, so happy to talk.

Even Dai Pen would talk to Ieuan. Dai was important; everybody said so. Dai was the head man in the village, and it was Dai that, four times a year, rode out to the Shire Council to represent the village alongside the other villages and towns. Dai knew how important he was in the village, but he also knew how unimportant the village was in the wider world. It was so difficult; everyone in the village expected Dai to fix anything that went wrong – after all, Dai was important – but Dai himself knew how little power he had; inside the village he had to get everyone to agree before anything would be done, and outside the village, well, he represented an obscure village at the end of a remote, unpaved road across the mountains, unimportant and largely forgotten. It made Dai feel so useless – and yet everyone said he was so important.

So Dai would talk to Ieuan, and tell him all this, and all about the Council, and the road, and the hills, and the things he wanted to do and couldn't, and Ieuan would listen, and maybe understand a little bit, but be so happy to listen and to talk to Dai, that in the end Dai's depression would lift, and he'd go away and try yet again to do something.

One thing Dai did want to fix was the road. There was only that one road in and out of the village, and it cut into the side of the hill for most of its length, climbing steadily for over two miles up to Blaen to meet the proper road from Aber to Glaswent. Because it was cut into the hill, stones and even quite big rocks were forever falling onto it, making it hard to ride a horse there, let alone get a cart along it. It was the big problem: it made it hard for farmers to get their lambs and their wool to market, and it made it hard for traders to visit the village. It held everything back, that road. But how to clear it – and more, how to keep it clear?

Then, suddenly, Dai thought of Ieuan. Ieuan could do it. It wasn't difficult, in the sense of understanding; Ieuan loved helping, and this was helping; could Ieuan do it? Dai spoke to Ieuan's Mam, and she thought he could, and that he'd enjoy it – and maybe it would do him good. Dai spoke to other people around the village, and they were happy. So Dai spoke to Ieuan.

Would he help pick up the stones from the road? Just from the village to Blean – no further – would he help?

Ieuan was very happy – he could help! Yes, Ieuan could help! Ieuan likes helping! Ieuan want to help!

And then Dai showed him where to dump the stones – in the old quarry by the turn to the Ros farm – and then gave Ieuan a barrow to carry the stones in. Not just lent – gave.

Ieuan's own barrow!

Ieuan had a barrow! He'd been trusted with a barrow of his own!

Ieuan had to tell everyone, to show everyone his barrow!

His Mam even had to let him take it into his bedroom at night, because it was his barrow, and he was so proud of it.

So, every day Ieuan would proudly trundle his barrow, Ieuan's barrow, along the road, picking up stones and putting them into his barrow, Ieuan's barrow, until it was full, then back to the quarry and tipping them in, and stopping to talk to everyone he met to show them his barrow, and tell them how happy he was to be useful, and to have his own barrow to be useful with.

And best of all, at the end of each week the village paid Ieuan a proper wage! Well, not really – it was pence not pounds, just to show appreciation – but it was enough for Ieuan to take home to give to his Mam like a proper son should. Ieuan was so proud. And so was his Mam.

And so was Dai. And so was the rest of the village – everybody liked Ieuan.

Dai still talked to Ieuan when they met. Dai would tell Ieuan all about his problems with the village and the Council, and Ieuan would tell Dai all about his barrow, and all about going along the road trundling his barrow and picking up stones and putting them into his barrow, and the noise they made as he tipped them into the quarry from his barrow. Then both would go away happier.

One day Dai happened to meet Ieuan just as he came to the old quarry, and they started talking as usual. But then Dai stopped.

'What are you doing, Ieuan?' he asked. 'Why are you picking out those stones? Don't they go into the quarry?'

'Pretty stones,' said Ieuan. 'Different stones. White pretty stones with yellow in them. Ieuan like pretty stones. Don't want to throw pretty stones in the quarry. Keep pretty stones here, in Ieuan's special place for pretty stones.'

And Ieuan showed Dai the special place where he'd sorted out the pretty stones, and Dai looked at the pieces of white quartz with tiny veins of yellow in them and wondered.

He wondered what the tiny veins of yellow were.

And above all, he wondered why no one else had noticed the pretty white stones with the yellow in them before Ieuan had.

'May I borrow a pretty stone, please, Ieuan?' he asked. 'I'll promise to bring it back.'

'Take pretty stone!' exclaimed Ieuan. 'Ieuan give pretty stone to Dai a present! Dai give Ieuan barrow, so Ieuan give Dai pretty stone as a present!'

'Thank you,' said Dai. 'You're very kind. And very clever to have seen that these stones are pretty. No one else has noticed – only Ieuan. Thank you.'

The assay wasn't wonderful, but it was gold, and it was enough to get a mining company interested. They opened an adit from the road, and as the custom was they called it after the mine company owner's wife – but that wasn't the name that stuck. Whatever the legal papers may have said, everyone, villagers, miners, mine company, everyone called it Ieuan's Barrow.

And Ieuan continued to potter along the road with his barrow, picking up rocks, and Dai continued to talk to him, and tell him all his problems – all his new problems, now his village had suddenly become rich and important – and still everyone expected Dai to do everything, and still everyone liked Ieuan, and Ieuan's Barrow was there to prove it.

And it still is.

The House on the Hill
by Joanne Stubbs

This story was inspired by a large, fragrant jasmine hedge in Tuscany.

There is an island where the sun rises twice a day. Its yellow limbs drift around the harbour, find a crack in the hillsides and stretch through, curious, before dipping again behind the granite knolls. For the villagers those first arms of light are a gentle warning – the day will soon break in earnest. The sun will slant up from the blue-edged cliffs and every little grey boat will bob against the water and come out white. The brown stones of the houses will soften to fawn, and the bees will roam the coast.

Amongst this, if you look, you will see children yawning, stretching their arms over their heads, stepping out of houses, and sniffing. They are the offspring of the town, brown hair and golden skin, mostly, and every morning this small group from the harbour walk to school together down winding tracks. As they go, the morning sun is warm on their foreheads and the cool air pulls at the hair on their arms. They taste salt in the sky and they chatter with hushed voices, tones matched to the placid morning waves. The shrill song of green plovers, shouting on the wing, follows them through the fields and their feet, some shoed, some bare, crush the edges of rosemary and lavender. The herbs were planted long before, by villagers, and have self-seeded into straggling trains of lilac and silver green. With every footstep the children send tiny clouds of scent into the air around them, but they smell nothing. Two generations was all it took for their sense of smell to disappear. It is a small island. And though they sniff – though their parents tell them stories of coffee and jasmine – their brains are as close to the smells around them as their heads are to the stars. That was life for them: no scent. Or it was, until they discovered the house on the hill.

It wasn't exactly that they discovered it – the children always knew the house was there – so much as they grew to know the magical powers of Mrs. Calathes, who spends late afternoons on her porch, eyes towards the horizon. From that seat, feet planted on wooden floorboards, elbows resting on polished chair arms, the old lady filters the work of the land through her hands. Beans are shelled, potatoes peeled, lemons squeezed. In late autumn, as the orange sun slants off the green ocean, she rolls one olive, maybe two, across her tongue and between her teeth. She picks them straight from the tree to test, day by day, their suppleness. She waits for the moment they are ready to press. When that day is nearly upon them she joins her husband in stretching soft green nets beneath the trees, ready for the fruit to drop. It is a small grove – ten trees only – but still, the couple aren't as young as they used to be, and it takes a full afternoon to unwrap the tangling traps and snake them beneath the branches. By evening her fingers ache. By mid-winter the crop will be down.

In summer, well before the olives grow fat, the couple busy themselves with honey. Mr. Calathes knows his bees – he treats them with love – and Mrs. Calathes knows her honey.

'You're the best bee-keeper on the island,' she says to him.

'I've had the most practice,' he returns, listening to the late afternoon buzz. Between the house and the olive grove is a wall of jasmine, thick with scent and humming with the beat of hundreds of wings.

'You make us sound ancient,' she says. 'We aren't dead yet.'

His mouth slants into a gentle smile. 'Not even close, my love.'

Each afternoon, movement draws Mr. Calathes' eyes to the bottom of the garden. Side-stepping through the garden gate and trotting up the sloped lawn, between the swathes of long grass, is a trickle of school children. This time there are four of them and their shadows are soft, their fingers splashed with ink, brains full of school. They chatter amongst themselves. Today, the first child waves and Mr. Calathes waves back, then sneaks a glance at his wife. He sees her head turned slightly, left ear pointing towards the children and the sea.

'Hello,' say the children as they reach the bottom steps of the porch.

'Hello, everyone,' says Mrs. Calathes, smiling. 'Come on up. How are you all?'

Each child answers as he or she climbs the steps, four voices scattering into the air like birdsong.

'How does the island smell today, Mrs. Calathes?' asks David, the leader of the pack. He has a scar across his right cheek – the last evidence of a tumble he took off a nearby cliff, aged five.

'Ah. Let me see,' says the old lady, tipping her nose to the sky and sniffing. Her eyes twinkle. 'What do you think Jac?' she says to her husband.

The children are seated now, legs crossed, and their eyes drift from the woman to her husband. They watch his thick brown moustache dance as he wrinkles his nose and purses his lips, taking in short, deep breaths.

'Sage,' he says. 'And butterfly wings.'

'Yes,' his wife agrees. 'And somewhere a bit further off, drifting along in the wind…fried mackerel.'

Elsa, the youngest, screws her face up in disgust. 'I don't like that,' she says. She has eyes the colour of umber and her brown hair falls straight down in thick velvet folds. She wraps a long, slender length of grass between her fingers as she speaks.

Mrs. Calathes opens her eyes wide. 'Oh. But maybe you'd like the way it smells.'

The little girl shakes her head.

'So what does it smell like?' David interrupts. With his rugged scar he is a formidable ten year old, earnest and curious. He asks the questions and looks the longest at the answers.

'The smells, ok, let's have a think,' says Mrs. Calathes. 'Sage, butterfly wings, and mackerel. Well. Sage is a full stomach – it's a slow walk up a gentle slope, and a warm jumper in a cool breeze. It's a rich, powerful smell that gets into every crevice of your brain and fills your head with a salty tang. It could be the King of the Herbs, don't you think, Jac?'

Her husband nods, his fingers pulling broad beans from fur-lined pods while his wife gives her lesson.

All four children sniff the air. 'What about the butterfly wings?' one asks.

Mrs. Calathes closes her eyes and takes a deep breath in through her nose. 'Ah, butterfly wings. They are a smell you have to concentrate on. You must focus. They smell like heart beats. So subtle, so delicate, but so vibrant. They are flashes of kingfisher blue. One moment they are with you, and the next they are gone. They smell like fresh, cold spring water.'

'And the mackerel?' asks Elsa. 'Does it smell the way it tastes?'

'Well, no, not exactly,' replies the old lady.

'Then maybe I could like it,' Elsa says.

Mrs. Calathes laughs. 'Well that's good. There's a lot to the smell of fried mackerel, you see. It's a particularly rich, complex smell. It's like waves hitting the backs of your calves at sunrise. It's also like a very strong ocean breeze against your face. It starts off being a cold smell, you see, and it gets hotter as it goes on, until it's a crisp, fire-hot smell. It's also that feeling you get when you run your fingers over the skin of a lemon. And at the end, just after you've swallowed, fried mackerel smells like a crash of saucepans in the middle of a busy kitchen.'

'I can almost smell it,' says David, head tilted to the side.

Mrs. Calathes thinks that, out of the corner of her eye, she sees her husband licking his lips.

'What about the honey?' asks one of the other children.

Mrs. Calathes nods. 'Well, you know it's honey season. But first – tell me about the island. What have you seen?'

This is an exchange that happens most days. The old lady tells the children everything she can about the scents on the air and in return they lend visions of the land. The paths they have scampered, the neighbourhood gatherings in the square behind the harbour, the birds in the sky and the fish in the blue sea. Mrs. Calathes knows this summer will be the last year she sees the honeybees – her eyes grow worse each day, her vision slowly clouding over.

The children describe a bird they saw on their walk to school: a black-tipped orange mane, long thin beak, striped wings. A hoopoe, they all decide. Mr. Calathes suggests that tomorrow the children try to spot its mate – they usually come in pairs – while his wife pushes herself slowly from her chair. She feels her joints creak as she straightens out.

'Time for the final smell?' she says, stepping through the open door and into the kitchen. The children stop talking and sit up a little straighter.

She returns with a jar filled with something cloudy, the colour of sandstone. Clutched along with it are five spoons, which she hands to the children before giving the fifth to her husband.

'The final smell of this summer's evening,' she says, lowering herself carefully back into her chair. 'Is honey. We creamed this jar last autumn. Everyone take a spoonful. And then wait, we're all going to eat together.'

She passes the jar to David and waits for each child to take one spoonful. Elsa is last and she looks bashful as she holds the honey out towards Mr. Calathes – his moustache is large; funny, when it's at a distance, but a bit scary up close. He tries not to grin too widely as he takes the tub from her little brown fingers.

'Now everyone, put the spoon in your mouth and don't swallow. Hold the honey on your tongue and close your eyes,' says Mrs. Calathes. She takes the jar from her husband and holds it beneath her nose. She inhales a lung full of honeyed scent and lets her mind drift off with the insects.

'Honey smells like the back legs of a bee,' she says. 'It smells like a blue sky and yellow sun, and the taste of sugar on the air. It smells, well, just like the taste in your mouth.'

She smiles and waves her left hand carelessly towards the children. 'Now off you go, everyone. I've got work to do.'

The children swallow, scatter their spoons and scramble away, laughing.

The boat arrives at dawn. Only this island would do such a thing – bring its visitors in the dark, to surprise them with its dual sunrise. David is caught off guard. Twilight shakes him by the collar twice over and he feels the first of a sense of long-lost familiarity settle upon his shoulders. He left the island when he was only twelve, in a summer of storms and endless rain. At least, that's what his parents always said, when they spoke of home. We left in a tempest. It has been sixty-three long years since then.

Stepping from the small boat, David turns his face to the rising sun, letting its warmth cover him. The scar on his right cheek is a shadow. His white hair, still thick, falls in rough folds about his ears. He takes a camera from its place over his left shoulder and frames a photo. He adjusts the focus, bringing the scene into clarity: the boats in the harbour, the blue green water, the brown stones beneath his feet. He tries to match the picture with the image in his memory.

Without pressing the shutter he lets the camera drop, back to the crook of his arm. He knew what he would find here.

Water slapping gently at the sides of vessels, mooring ropes creaking, gulls squawking, children chattering on their walk to school. The fishermen would stand here, on this spot that he stands, and gossip. But everything feels a little different now. He lets the air fill his lungs, breathing in this new place. His hearing is not as it was; he no longer relies on it. These days, he uses his nose.

David was in his early fifties when the first major advances in gene therapy were made. He knew nothing of it. At that point, there were things more pressing; the therapies went to cancer patients, or to treat severe genetic disorders. So David was well into his sixties before his sense of smell was considered. By that point the therapies had been honed and sculpted by ten years of trials; when his personalised medicine finally came, the side effects of delivery were minimal, and the endurance of the therapy exceptional. At sixty-five years of age, David finally smelled the world.

He turns, bending carefully, and picks the hold-all up from beside his feet, shouldering it next to his camera. The other boat passengers are gone now, disappeared into homes and hillsides. He traces the line of the wall, past the fishermen's cottages, up the stone slope, beyond the mooring ropes, and into the depths of the bay. Here the grassy hillsides slope down towards the sea and there is a bench set, just as before, beneath the dripping arms of a wall of jasmine. He can smell it – yes, smell it – many metres before he takes a seat. It is luxurious and unignorably potent.

David drops his bag and places his camera on the bench. His nose is full, his head so steeped in the perfume that his eyes begin to water. Each small white flower is a star on a backdrop of deep green; he imagines the scent rising in plumes. Beneath the greenery, poking out here or there, is the soft, crumbling stone wall on which it grows. As a child he would sit here and wait for his father's boat to return to harbour each evening. He would reach his hand into the jasmine and run his fingertips along the cool edges of the wall, searching for crumbling pieces and pulling them free. The thought of doing this now astonishes him – it would be overwhelming to reach into that scented mass. He holds in a sneeze. What a smell. He had no idea, those years before, that it was so dizzyingly sweet.

He lets himself sit, watching the sun track upwards in the sky. Finally, he stands and picks up his things. He turns to the west, beginning to follow the route out of the harbour which he used to walk to school. The sun is hot now and the light glances off the sea. As he begins the climb out of the bay his breathing quickens; beneath his old legs the slope is steep, but it is shorter than he remembers. He reaches the brow of the hill and stops to take in the view, scents of lavender and rosemary catching in his lungs.

In the distance, some way along the path, he sees the house on a hill. It is sheltered from view slightly by the olive grove that grows beside it, so that only its terracotta roof is visible. Despite this, David knows that a long porch runs the length of the back of the house; that there are three steps up to it and that its wooden floorboards are worn smooth and comfortable from years of use. From there the view extends across the garden, beyond the spot where beehives always sat, and out over the open sea. From that porch the waves are green, and only choppy when the wind is high. The sun starts its day at the front of the house and ends with its long rays on the porch.

As he approaches, David sees nets strung out beneath the olive trees. A young woman sits on the porch, a book in her hands. The hinges of the garden gate squeak as David presses against it, and the woman looks up.

She stands, shielding her eyes from the low sun. 'Hello,' she calls.

David introduces himself. 'It has been a very long time since I was here,' he says, gesturing towards the house. 'I used to know the old couple that lived here.'

The woman smiles. Her hair is a crown of black velvet, pulled into a pile at the top of her head. 'My great-grandparents lived here,' she says. 'Many years ago. The place was empty for a good long while, after they passed away.'

'Oh,' says David. 'Your great-grandparents. You're a Calathes then?'

Rosa Calathes, she says her name is. She watches David with curiosity. 'You knew my great-grandparents then?' she asks.

'Oh yes. Your great-grandmother, Mrs. Calathes – she was something of a wizard to us children. I have very fond memories of her.'

Briefly, he tells Rosa about their afternoon lessons. The smells, the spoonful's of honey, and the slow insistent drop of broad beans into the bowl in Mr. Calathes' lap. 'But I can smell now,' he finishes, with a small shrug. 'They cured me.'

'Goodness,' says Rosa. 'And how is the world? It must be so different.'

He smiles. 'It's like an old friend with a new story.'

'How beautiful,' she laughs. Without another word she holds up her finger and disappears into the house. She returns with a jar full of sandstone coloured liquid and two spoons.

'Take a seat,' she says, beckoning to David. 'I'm afraid I don't have any bees yet. This is from the other side of the island, but it will have to do.'

She twists the lid off and hands the jar to him.

Dipping his spoon in, David breathes in the scent of the rich, earthy liquid.

'How is it?' Rosa asks a moment later, her own mouth full of honey.

'Best in the world.'

She laughs. 'Is it wonderful to come back here and finally be able to smell all of this?' she says.

He hands the jar back to her and takes a deep breath, eyes

closed, to see how different this place is. Sage, jasmine and olive blossom come to him first, followed by the tang of the ocean.

'I've been travelling a lot, seeking out the places of my past,' he says. 'Sometimes, finding the smells can actually make me feel like a stranger in a place I thought I knew. Mostly, yes, it is wonderful. But here? Nothing is different. It's exactly as I remember. Maybe this was the only place I could always smell.'

DUN I

By Alison Jackson

(Pronounced 'dun ee' – this is the highest point on Iona.)

This is a thin place, they say, where earth and heaven meet,
as light shines translucent on land and sea and sky
and sky and ocean merge as one in shades of azure blue.

The islands here are indigo above their silver shores,
where shifting sand and breakers pay homage to the sun.
Staffa, Lunga, Fladda, Coll, Tiree and Dutchman's Cap.

Yellow gorse absorbs the sun, then breathes out coconut.
The homely hum of insects among familiar flowers
belies the scent of distant lands where this same ocean runs.

A lark sings overhead, a lamb cries for the ewe and, finding her,
it sucks her milk, tail twirling like a top. Along the shore
gulls shriek and soar while oystercatchers pipe and probe.

In this thin place of beauty and of light, it's easy to have faith,
to believe in something more. But this is not my place; I must
go home
where light is harsh, the pavements hard, creation firmly
tamed.

But still defiant flowers grow between the pavement flags;
foxes scavenge rubbish bins; fierce falcons nest on office
blocks;
sparrows bathe in gutter dust; gulls flock on rubbish dumps.

And now when I shall see those things, beyond them too I'll
see
these birds, and gorse, and islands, and sunlight on the sea,
and light will shine translucent as my home grows thin for me.

The French Bride
by Jane Gray-Wallis

This is an extract from a longer piece. It concerns the marriage of a French Princess to an English Prince. The matter of the consummation of the marriage is proving to be a problem, not just for the married couple.

John is preparing the King for bed or at least he is trying to do so. The King is pacing the bed chamber. He has dismissed his other staff who have hurried away bearing trays and a chamber pot. As the King passes, John tries to help him out of his gown. Each time his hand is shrugged away. On the sixth pass the King stops abruptly 'Christ!' he says, as if he means it. 'I have only been away for four weeks!' John waits … 'Let me understand clearly' says the King. 'The longed for consummation of this marriage by the Prince, has not actually happened? The Princess and her esteemed lady Cecile tricked my son into believing that he had indeed performed. So, there is still to be no child.'

John nods, he looks down at the floor.

'And you colluded in this? How exactly?'

'Chicken Sire. From the kitchen', he adds.

'I know where a chicken comes from.' The King folds his arms and waits.

John sighs. 'He spoke to the Princess of an annulment. As luck would have it, he also mentioned it to the Queen. She would have none of it and sent him to a lady for training. A professional lady but high born. A lady who serves the aristocracy if you take my meaning. It was in utmost secrecy Sire.'

'And …?' says the King.

'No luck Sire. He truly doesn't feel attracted to women. The Princess is terrified that she will be sent back to France. She would, of course, be overjoyed to see her father again but the French King would undoubtedly take a dim view of his niece being sent home in shame.'

The King sinks into a chair and puts his head in his hands. 'It's worse than I thought.'

John is more optimistic. 'Not so Sire, for the Prince now believes he has consummated his marriage. All talk of annulment is gone. The Queen is happy, the Prince relieved, the court is in a much more up lifted mood. Perhaps in time, believing he has done it once before, the Prince may yet find himself capable.'

'But, with a Virgin wife, no possibility of a child.'

John moves his head and purses his lips, 'not at the present moment Sire, no.'

'Give me strength.' The King leans back in his chair and sighs.

John draws a stool up to the King's chair and begins to help him on with his bed socks. 'There is something we could try', he says. 'It's complicated so you will have to hear me out.' He leans forward and speaks in a low voice. 'You remember when I was with his Lordship in charge of the stables.'

'Of course I remember' says the King. It has always been a particular pleasure to him that he was able to take the Earl of Norfolk's treasured stud man right away from under his nose.

'His Lordship had a mare. Possibly he has her still. She wouldn't take to the stallion. Wouldn't let him near. Rearing, kicking, a right carry on. Of course, we hobbled her and had the twitch on her lip but when we brought the stallion forward she reared up so high we thought she would brain herself on the cross beam or come over backwards and kill herself. We were in a fine fettle I can tell you. She was a very beautiful mare, very fast and valuable. His Lordship *would* breed from her. He wouldn't brook 'no' for an answer. So anyway, she was quiet for us to handle so we decided to help out.'

The King looks up. 'What did you do?'

The next day we got a couple of trestles and threw the mare's rug over them. We kept her standing by with the twitch on and then well, the stallion he was quite eager, as before and well ....

'Well what ..?'

'I'm getting to that ...well we led him up and he mounted up his front quarters on the trestle and well we ... we ... we collected 'is contribution. We had a jug, we put it in that.' John shrugs.

The King is staring at John who hurries on with his narrative.

'Well, she was docile with us, the mare so we, well the other stud groom, he made a sort of channel with his hand, at her passage so to speak, and we tipped it in.'

'And now you are going to tell me she had a beautiful foal eleven months later.'

'To the day Sire!' says John triumphantly. 'Same again two years later. His Lordship was very pleased. Not that he ever knew how his mare was covered.'

'And the point of this outrageous story is ...'

'Well Sire, if it can work with a horse then why not a Prin ... err a person?'

The King is silent, colour rises in his cheeks. He clenches his jaw. With a flicker of dismay John sees his position crumbling and, along with that, his job at court. 'The situation was desperate.' he says, 'If I hadn't got that mare in foal I would have lost mi job.'

'Even if this is possible, which I don't believe for a moment, how on earth do you propose to present the idea to the Prince or to the Princess?' He pauses. 'It is nonsense,' he says finally. 'Now be away before I charge you with treason.'

John is only too glad to go.

Later, as the King brings himself to a climax, he looks down and wonders at the ludicrousness of the whole idea.

John lies in a narrow bed under the eaves and wonders. He stares at the ceiling without really seeing it. The key to the whole operation will be the lady Cecile, of that he has no doubt.

Eventide
By Ann Revill

'I'm so sorry, Mrs. Jenkins. It's really embarrassing.' Joan, the stout care assistant Molly Jenkins privately called 'The Elephant', hesitated on the threshold.

'Come in, dear. What is it?'

'It's Mr. Reynolds – he's made a complaint.'

'Yes?' Molly Jenkins smiled encouragingly.

'He says you – well – showed him some photos.' The Elephant's ears were turning crimson.

'Photos?' Molly's eyes turned vaguely towards the family album on her bedside table.

'No, not those. Naughty photos.'

'Naughty?'

'Obscene.' The Elephant blushed to the tip of her trunk.

Molly's hand went to her chest. Her breathing fluttered. 'What are you saying, my dear? Do you really think that likely? Mr. Reynolds was in here yesterday. We had a chat, but there were certainly no photos!'

'I'm sorry. But Matron said I should have a look in your room.'

'A search?' Molly's expression was something between affront and amusement. Difficult to maintain for long. 'Well, certainly, dear, if it will make you feel any better. Perhaps you should check Mr. Reynolds' room too.'

The Elephant made a perfunctory venture into the chest of drawers, while Molly, relaxing her face into a mood of genteel injury, carefully concealed her handbag beneath her lap rug.

Having a room next to the bathroom was convenient. It was difficult to move quickly with the arthritis, but Molly was able to hear when Tightpants turned the water off. His footsteps passed her door as he went to collect John Reynolds for his ten o'clock bath. Molly reached the bathroom in a few moments. She was able to add about a gallon from the hot tap to the tub, before she had to throw herself on to the toilet seat, just as Tightpants arrived with his charge.

'No, no, my fault entirely. I should have remembered to lock the door.' Brushing aside their profuse apologies, she hobbled out to wait in the corridor until she heard John Reynolds shout as his feet dipped into the scalding water. Breathing a contented sigh, Molly made her way to his room. Carefully she placed the photos at the back of his bookshelf; the corner of one was just visible between the volumes. She would have to send for some more after a week or so.

Molly had resisted, for as long as she could, the insistence that she should join the trip to Clevedon.

'You'll really enjoy it, Mrs. Jenkins. I bet it's an age since you went to the seaside!'

Five years ago in Tenerife, to be exact. A slow crawl along the windswept seafront with the other geriatrics from the Mercy Whittaker Eventide Home was not Molly's idea of entertainment. However, since Mr. Reynolds was the only one staying behind after the banning order imposed by Matron, she realised that it would probably be in her interest to give in gracefully.

'I just didn't want to hold you all up,' she murmured.

Reassured that there would be wheelchairs for all when needed, she smiled gratefully. 'You take such good care of us!'

The sky was satisfactorily threatening when their coach parked on the front. With luck a downpour might start a couple of cases of pneumonia. That would ease the congestion in the Eventide Home Day Room.

'I think I'll try a wheelchair,' she said to the Elephant, as the party passed through the ornamental gates of the pier. 'No, no, I can manage myself. You push someone who needs more help.'

It was not hard to get into the knack of manoeuvring the appliance. She took a brisk run along the length of the pier for practice, then began the return journey. Meeting the party strolling towards her, she adopted a frown of concentration, adroitly managing to skirt most of the group. Unfortunately, she caught one foot of Mrs. Robinson's Zimmer frame at the last moment, toppling her to the deck with a crash. Molly heard no crack of bone, but nevertheless could not rest content until Mrs. Robinson had been wheeled in her own chair to the exit to await the ambulance.

'I can easily manage with my stick. So careless of me. I should have taken Joan's advice in the first place.'

'Now then, Mrs. Jenkins.' The Elephant patted her hand. 'Don't distress yourself. Accidents can happen to anyone. I'm sure Mrs. Robinson will be all right. Just a bruise or two. Now, you didn't hurt yourself, did you? Do you want me to take you back to the coach?'

Molly protested that she could easily continue the walk along the pier. She leant exceptionally heavily on the Elephant's arm.

Only the relatively mobile could make their way through the crowded display shelves of the pier shop.

‘Can I help, Miss Foster?’ Molly stretched to reach down a postcard from the top of a carousel. She was able, at the same time, to slip an expensive-looking plaque into Miss Foster’s bag. ‘Anything else you’re interested in? What about those lace handkerchiefs?’

When Miss Foster protested that she couldn’t really afford such a luxury, Molly made sure that a couple of packets joined the plaque, leaving an obvious gap on the counter.

The shop assistant caught up with them halfway back to the coach, as it was beginning to rain. There was a mortifying session of bag-searching. Miss Foster, questioned severely by Matron, ‘Mother’s Ruin’, dissolved into tears, becoming totally incoherent when she pointed out Molly.

‘Don’t shift the blame on to Mrs. Jenkins,’ snapped Mother’s Ruin. ‘She is the most co-operative of all of you. Give the goods back at once.’

It was decided to curtail the visit as the heavens now opened. Dripping, the elderly trippers were assisted on to the coach. Molly leaned back serenely in her seat, smiling sympathetically at the sobbing Miss Foster. She unwrapped one of the chocolates she had picked up in the shop. All in all, the outing had been, as promised, profitable and entertaining. Perhaps she might join next month’s treat – a boat trip to Lundy Island.

The Montage Year
By Caroline Bennett

After the films Rocky, Flashdance, Working Girl, Overboard.

This is the year of my montage.
I shall run up all the steps in Philadelphia without stopping for breath
Raising my arms in the air at the top,
Pausing only to be drenched with cold water
In Pittsburgh, while dancing into the night like a maniac
After working my shift, welding at the steel mill,
Before heading off to fall overboard while diving for oysters
In Elk Cove, Oregon
I pick up my four kids from school
Who raise turtles in the sink and superglue my hands to plates
But I love them anyway
And I keep on going
Because I've gotta catch the Staten Island Ferry to Manhattan
Where I change my sneakers into high heels
To match my big hair and my shoulder pads
And make connections in the newspaper clippings
And pull all-nighters and spray champagne
On all those haters
Until I get my corner office.

Struggling Against the Elements

By Alan Shrimpton

This piece was written in response to a very simple exercise that simply gave everyone the same phrase – 'Struggling Against the Elements' – and invited them to construct a short story around that theme. There is, of course, a twist in the tail of this story.

For the umpteenth time that evening, David raged at the unexpected snowfall that had made driving a miserable test of concentration for the last hour. With the light fading, and snow falling ever faster, David turned carefully off the main road onto the lane that led to the cottage.

The windscreen wipers thumped backwards and forwards in a vain attempt to keep the glass clear but David couldn't decide whether it was better to have them on slow and attempt to peer through the thickening layer of flakes, or fast and make the whole windscreen smeary. He opted for slow.

Why, he wondered angrily, couldn't it have waited another hour or two to start snowing? Being snowed into the cottage with Beth for the weekend would have been perfect. There were two bulging Waitrose shopping bags and a half case of mixed wines on the back seat, and he knew the log store was full. Yes, he thought, snow in two hours' time would have been more idyllic. But instead, he thought, there was a real risk that he might not even get there. He didn't have the right clothes to walk the last couple of miles.

As if in response to that thought, the wind picked up and began to drive the snow hard into the windscreen, his headlights reflecting back from a thickening wall of flakes. Hi-beam wasn't helping so he dipped the lights and drove still slower. He hoped that Beth had got away earlier than him and made it to the cottage. For a moment, his mind wandered onto log fires, wine, and Beth wearing… well not much actually.

He found himself smiling for the first time in over a hour. He was still smiling as the last bend in the lane, hidden by the combination of slow wipers and dipped headlights, loomed out of the snow. The slow crash into the gate was unavoidable and expensively noisy.

'Buggar,' cried David with some vehemence, and then laid tongue to rather cruder expressions of his frustration, thumping the steering wheel for good measure. The car bumped to a stop in the field and the engine stalled. David said 'buggar' again, louder this time.

When he failed to beat the steering wheel into lots of small pieces, he calmed down enough to realise that he was less than half a mile from the cottage, and that, appropriate clothing or not, he could probably manage that even with his bag and the shopping. He could leave the wine and come back for it. Beth would have bought some anyway. Beth's image sprang to mind again, and he decided that they could live without the wine for an evening if they really had to. He turned on the hazard lights, grabbed the bags and climbed out of the car.

Ten minutes later, walking directly into the wind and plastered with snow, that didn't seem to be such a good idea. For a moment he even wondered if he was lost or had blundered past the cottage and was walking away from it, but then he thought of Beth and trudged onwards. He couldn't feel his hands now, except where the carrier bag straps were cutting into his fingers, but he knew he must be close. That had been the last bend before the cottage so it must be just ahead he thought. Head down, trying to blink the snow out of his eyes, he ploughed on.

And suddenly he was there… but Beth wasn't. No car on the drive and the cottage was dark. His heart sank as numb fingers fumbled the key into the lock and pushed the door open. No matter, he thought, she can't be far behind. Just get the fire going and some lights on then… His phone chirped and he dropped the bags, still halfway through the door, and fished the thing out of his pocket. But it wasn't a call, just a voice mail. From Beth.

He pressed play. She must have pulled over to let the snow die-down and wanted to let him know where she was, he thought.

'David,' her voice said. 'I'm very sorry but I think my husband suspects something. I don't think it's safe to see each other this weekend so I'm not coming…. I'm really sorry. Probably best with all this snow though. I'll call you on Monday, but I hope…'

The rest of the message went unheard as David hurled the phone out into the snow. Which quickly covered it.

To the Garden Centre and Beyond

By Nastasya (Tia) Parker

My smile feels like glue. I'm afraid to peel it off. Nell, my ex, doesn't notice because she's tearing around, throwing toys, clothes, and juice cartons into an Octonaut-shaped bag.

The baby sees my expression, though. She's staring at me. I call Gloria a baby – she's more than two now. Probably smarter than me already.

Nell's fiancé patters down the stairs. 'Thanks for covering while we do this wedding taster.' He sounds like a car salesman, the heartiness in his voice as real as my smile.

'Happy to,' I say, in case my face isn't showing that.

Baby Gloria's puffed up like a marshmallow in a pink parka, her arms stiffly angled from her sides. Nell grabs a cardigan and then Gloria, while her salesman checks the shine on his shoes. Then they all look at me.

Right. They don't want me unsupervised in their Ikea showroom of an apartment. They're just too polite to say so, if you call the flaming evils Nell gives me polite.

Fair enough, after all I've put Nell through. Blush-heat melts the smile off my face, and I follow them outside.

Helpless, I watch Nell buckle Gloria's seat into the back of my old Corsa. Then off she goes with the guy who, let's face it, might as well be Gloria's dad, in a Passat as shiny as his shoes. I sit in my driver's seat, clinging to the worn steering wheel, craning my neck to stare back at my daughter.

'Wanna go to the garden centre?' I ask. It's what 'normal' people do, my workmates have said. 'We can see the pets there, and the fountains, maybe get some cake. Yeah?'

She doesn't speak, just looks.

I rummage in the passenger footwell for my favourite Avengers comic. My cellmate got me hooked on them. If you think those good versus evil plots are unrealistic, you haven't battled addiction like I have. 'Wanna read?'

She takes it without turning from my face. Her cute button nose quivers, launching a green bogey.

I leap into frenzied action. 'A tissue! Where's a tissue?' I find a hanky in the glove compartment, to intercept the snot invasion.

But I stop short with the hanky inches from her face. Am I allowed to touch her? To my baby, I must look like a monster out of Marvel's pages, with spiky hair, and tattoos creeping from my collar and sleeves. 'Take it.' I wave the hanky like a white flag. 'Wipe up.'

Her fingers, almost as pink as her jacket, curl around the tissue, and she splats it to her face. The Hulk-coloured stuff disappears.

'You do talk, right?' I ask her. 'I swear I remember you talking.'

They let me take her out once before, when she was still one, right after I found a job. I took her to see my work; thought the big lorries would impress her. Gloria babbled in the car, squealed at the trucks, and covered herself in chocolate my new workmates gave her.

Nell said that made me an even worse dad than before. 'That smell—ugh! Marcus, how could you let a baby spend the day with bin men?'

We prefer the term *Sanitation Implementation Assistants.*

And today Gloria doesn't make a peep. She was only three months old when I was drunk out of my head and bruised

Nell's collarbone with a saucepan. But I'd thought I was on the right track since then. The way the baby looks at me now, Nell must be right.

'Maybe you'd like the park better,' I suggest. 'We could play outside…' A fat, arrogant berk of a raindrop hits the windscreen, its mates following after. 'Great. Maybe not.'

I'm sweating and I want a drink. I get out my phone—my best alternative to alcohol, apart from comic books—and open the Music app. 'Let's have some songs, hey?' The Samsung pretends to load my options, but nothing happens. It's as bad as Gloria. 'Come on…'

There's a rustling behind me. Still staring, Gloria wiggles from side to side in that straitjacket Nell's zipped her into. She speaks Japanese or something, as if hypnotised: 'Konkwo, Konkwo, Akinaw…'

'Holy—' I bite back swears. My toddler is possessed!

'Hawa Honda Wachuwa…'

Then I realise she's singing 'Twinkle, Twinkle, Little Star.' My baby heard me talking about songs, so she's doing me a show. 'Beautiful, sweetheart! What a clever girl.'

She smiles, opens the comic book, and commands me, 'Go vroom.'

I drive real slow. This little box hasn't got one of those stickers like Nell has: *Baby on Board*. I don't know if it's legal to drive the kid without one.

We head out of town. Gloria rattles the comic pages and narrates her own sound effects: 'Pow! Swoosh!' She's pretty good.

In the car park, I battle Gloria's seat. It's got straps everywhere. I peel off one and find another, then another. Her coat creaks as I struggle, and finally she's free—now what?

'Uh…wanna come out?' I ask her.

Her arms twitch up. She doesn't let go the comic book. I lean down and carefully lift her. She's light, despite the pink parka armour. I'm doing it! I got this!

'Trucks?' suggests Gloria hopefully as I carry her inside.

'Ah…No, baby, but we can see some cute little animals.'

The pet corner is toward the back. Gloria clings to my neck, the Avengers flapping behind my ears in her grasp, as I take her past candles that smell of a bakery, and a bakery that smells of bleach. The plants smell of water. I carry her through the jungle of potted plants, imagining we're on a mission, out to save the world.

We find the fish. I let her down and make a fishy face at her. My secret agent breaks cover, shrieking with laughter. I glance around, terrified people will think I'm torturing her. A couple of old ladies smile over an array of flowerpots, and a big, bearded bloke in a high-vis vest chuckles, looking up from soil sacks.

With Gloria beside me, people ignore my tattoos, seeing I have something to offer apart from collecting their weekly rubbish. I don't have to pretend I'm a superhuman in disguise, because as a dad, I'm actually human.

At the rabbit and guinea pig hutches, Gloria coos like a doting granny. Nell must be teaching her to be gentle. You don't learn much of that from comics; I don't know if I've got it in me. Standing over my daughter, I reach out, a tattooed serpent's tail showing on the back of my hand, and I touch Gloria's soft curls. I'm so careful she doesn't even notice. That's my role, I think. I'll be your Dark Knight, baby girl. Ready to save you but destined to stay hidden most of the time.

She scampers to the water features, shouting, 'Splash! Splash!' I catch her by her flapping pink hood and guide her to approach with caution. Crouching beside the biggest fountain, we dip our hands in together. She turns mine over and traces the tattoo up under my sleeve with her dripping, chubby fingers. I'm holding my breath. She finds the snake's head, hisses in my ear, and laughs. My knees give way. This girl is my kryptonite.

Coral Reef
by Anne Sheppard

The inspiration for this poem came from the last sentence of a book, written on a slip of paper that I chose randomly at one of the Writers Group meetings. The exercise was to use it as the first sentence of a piece of writing. Because of copyright law I have changed it slightly.

Here in this jewelled space between the bitterness of land
And the whispering blue of the South Pacific sky,
Lies that magnificence of nature's blending,
Where currents masquerade as limp dark pools
Only revealed, as vagabonding eddies race
To sweep the starfish from their perch;
While coral hard and brittle scrape their feet
As down they go, through myriads of towers
And waving tree-like ferns bereft of spores.
This beautiful yet lost and lonely place,
The home and prison of all found here.
Alluring in its serenity, ugly in its uncouth roughness,
Where death lurks in every crevice
And passion, if found at all, will never reveal its joyful face -
Only its necessity for procreation.

Author Biographies

Joan Bartholomew

At the time of writing, Joan is Wotton Writers Group's newest recruit. She moved to Wotton from north Wales in March 2022. Previously, Joan attended a weekly writers group in Mold, Flintshire. She writes articles about her eccentric family. Joan is a retired English teacher. Her hobby is collecting knife rests which began when she lived in France. Her muse is a very small Yorkshire terrier called Typin.

Dave Beer

Dave grew up in an RAF family so moved around a great deal in childhood, starting his schooldays in Iraq. He and his wife Alison have lived in Surrey, North Nibley, and Scotland. They returned to North Nibley in 2006 when Dave retired from his career as a nuclear engineer. He studied creative writing through Stroud College Outreach programme in the 1990s and helped form the Nailsworth Writing Group. Dave joined Wotton Writers Group on his return to Gloucestershire. His work is strongly inspired by his experiences travelling in wild and lonely places. He also enjoys writing science fiction and horror stories.

Caroline Bennett

Caroline grew up in South Wales, works in the environmental sector and has a side hustle selling vintage books. Since childhood she has written stories and poems but shoved them in shoe-boxes under the bed. She has lived in Wotton under Edge since 2009. She wrote a novel once but found it so exhausting she decided it might not be for her. She knits, reads obsessively, and writes mostly poetry outside of writers group. Caroline enjoys the challenge of writing something on command in Wotton Writers Group and seeing what her brain can come up with under pressure.

Jane Gray-Wallis

Twenty-five years ago Jane was one of the founding members of Wotton Writers Group. Throughout her years in the group she has enjoyed the camaraderie, support, and helpful comments, plus lots of laughs. Jane is a coppicer, spoon carver and teaches woodcraft. She previously worked for the BBC Natural History Unit and has a life-long passion for traditional country skills and nature. When not wielding a chainsaw Jane writes for pleasure, finding a devil-may-care attitude liberates the subconscious. She writes romance, comedy, and drama. She published a children's book – Auntie Meg and the Dragon, in the nineties.

Alan Jackson

Alan came to Wotton-under-Edge in 1978, working as a mathematician in heavy engineering and in nuclear power. Jane Gray-Wallis introduced Alan to the Writers' Group not long after it started – he was surprised how much he enjoyed it. He has never really tried to get published but had a story highly commended in a Stroud competition, and had a couple of pieces published in an anthology. Alan writes observational humour, science fiction, fantasy, and historical pieces.

Alison Jackson

Alison Jackson is a retired civil servant whose career involved writing a large number of documents – briefing papers, press notices, speeches and even parts of Government White Papers! She thoroughly enjoyed this, relishing the need to adapt her style to the requirements of each type of document. She still enjoys the challenge of writing to a brief and her pieces in this collection reflect this. Her favourite place in the world is the west coast of Scotland, particularly the island of Iona. She enjoys travel, with a particular interest in the history and wildlife of the places she visits.

Tim Melling

Tim has been writing for 30 years, mostly for his work – articles, research etc. He has been full of good intentions about practising the craft, but work has always got in the way. When he retires …. A Lancastrian by birth, he has lived in Liverpool, London and, for the last 33 years, in Gloucestershire. He is married with 3 children and four young grandchildren and is beginning to feel his age. A keen cyclist he rode the route of the tour de France for charity a few years ago and can often be seen gasping up some of the steep Cotswold climbs.

Nastasya (Tia) Parker

Tia joined Wotton Writers Group 18 years ago when she first emigrated from the USA to Gloucestershire. She now lives in Dursley and works in the secondary school there. Her contemporary literary fiction, often honed using feedback from the group, has appeared in two Bristol Short Story Prize and two Stroud Short Story anthologies, a Retreat West anthology, Perhappened Magazine, and The Phare. In 2017, she won the Gloucestershire Writers' Network Prose Prize. She is editing her irreverent novel giving Eve's perspective on the creation myth and blogging about the random stories we find in daily life, at http://nastasyaparker.com/.

Anna Quartly

Anna is the youngest member of Wotton Writers Group at eighteen years old. She is home-educated and is just starting college. During her home education Anna achieved a Grade A in her AFA Creative Writing course in one year instead of the usual two. Anna's poetry has been published in Iceberg Tales, the Wotton Times, Bind, and Ramblers GB. She has been writing poetry and prose for the past three years inspired by the beauty of nature on Cotswold walks. Anna is also a member of a book group in Wotton and has performed multiple times at an event called Re-Verse with other poets in Malmesbury Abbey. She can be found on twitter @AnnaQuartly

Ann Revill

Ann was born in South London in 1936. After starting her education in a tiny 'Dame School', she entered Watford Grammar School for Girls. Anne went on to study History at St. Anne's College, Oxford. In the John Wesley Society, she met Philip who she went on to marry. They have two sons, born while they lived in Salisbury in the 1960s. Ann taught at Portsmouth Girls Grammar School, Honor Oak School in London, Downend Comprehensive, and Page School for Girls. There she became Head of Humanities and Head of Upper School. Taking voluntary redundancy was an opportunity for Ann to teach part time while beginning to research a book she had been longing to write for many years, about the life of the Elizabethan astrologer, Doctor John Dee. A later effort on the life of Frances Coke in the reign of James I, was published due to the generosity and inspiration of Alan Shrimpton and the Wotton Writers Group.

Anne Sheppard

Originally from Nottinghamshire, Anne grew up on a diet of Robin Hood, Sherwood Forest, and poetry. She studied agriculture and bookkeeping and has been self-employed as a farm secretary/bookkeeper since 1971 when she moved to Gloucestershire. Anne has a diverse range of interests, including dowsing, genealogy, spirituality, and meditation. She is also a Reiki Master. Anne has one book published, The Purple

Hare's Guide to Inspirational Writing. Her poetry has been published in several magazines including a prize winner in Sentinel Magazine. She has also written articles for Writing Magazine and Mind, Body, and Spirit Magazine. Anne has two children and two grandchildren. More information can be found on her website www.inspiredtowrite.co.uk

Alan Shrimpton
After a lifetime of technical writing, and now most recently editing a quarterly aviation journal, Alan has spent the last 30 years happily exploring creative writing through courses, writing festivals, author's evenings, books and the Wotton Writers Group. And whilst he has had nothing published yet, or even won a competition, the time spent writing has been fun and full of companionship, which is more than enough reason to do it. When not trying to write, Alan may be found on his beloved narrowboat or walking one of England's national trails. Alan lives just outside Wotton where he cooks and enjoys good wine with friends.

Joanne Stubbs
Joanne grew up in Staffordshire. She moved to Wotton under Edge following a number of years living and working in Bristol. She joined Wotton Writers Group in 2020. She holds an MA in Creative Writing from Bath Spa University, and her debut novel, The Fish, was published in 2022 by Fairlight Books. Set in a dystopian near future, The Fish imagines a world in which fish start to crawl out of the polluted oceans and adapt to live on land. www.fairlightbooks.co.uk/the-fish

Lightning Source UK Ltd.
Milton Keynes UK
UKHW022021091122
411908UK00012B/355

9 781782 229650